A Riverman's Legacy

&

Other Ozark Tales

Rick Mansfield

A Riverman's Legacy & Other Ozark Tales

Copyright 2017 by Eric "Rick" Mansfield

All rights reserved.

No part of this publication may be reproduced, distributed or transmitted in any form, or by any means including but not limited to photocopying and internet; without the prior written consent of the author except in the case of brief quotations embodied in critical reviews and certain other noncommercial uses as defined by copyright law.

Dedication

Buck Maggard

September 1, 1906---July 19, 20

Gaylord Eugene "Buck" Maggard was born shortly after the start of the 20th century near Houston, Missouri to Fernando and Louisa Maggard ; one of eight children. In 1935 he married Loreen Purcell in Herman, to where the two then moved. Loreen's family, the Purcells, had first moved to the area around 1868.

They later moved to Grand Junction, Colorado where they raised and trucked vegetables and fruit throughout Colorado and Nebraska. In 1948 they moved back home to Akers and purchased Loreen's father's farm and business. Loreen served as Post Mistress as they operated a post office within the general store, as well as ran the ferryboat in northern Shannon County. Along with running the farm, Buck owned a sawmill and in the early years worked at the Medlock Stone Company. He helped in the store, often cutting hair as the local barber. Both were quite active in community and church affairs, belonging first to the Mt. Zion Church and later to the Corinth Baptist Church.

Beginning first by outfitting johnboat float trips and then in 1955 they started a campground and canoe rental. Initially a venue of only four canoes, their business grew to a fleet of more than two hundred. Eventually turning the running of the business over to their son Eugene, Buck always loved the river and had a deep affection for all that shared that emotion. Quick with a joke and a story, he enjoyed visiting with old friends as well as new visitors. Played the fiddle at local square dances. Along with his congeniality, he is best remembered for his love of the river itself.

Table of Contents

A Cargo Predestined	11
Blood Red	19
The Table	28
The Picture	34
Grandpa's New Book	37
The Bucket List	43
The Blizzard Brunch	46
The Gift	56
Check # 1817	61
What's In A Name?	69
The Pay Check	71
Grandma's New Pet	75
A Half Century of Hunting Tails	78
American Heroes: The Jack Roberts Episode	81
A Riverman's Legacy	86
The Stand	90
The Check	93
Healing Waters	99
Fifty Dollars	111
The Deadline	120
The Pavilion	123
The Legend of Ol' 95	132
The Ghost Mule	142
Secrets of Horse Hollow	147

A Casket's True Calling	159
The Pie Supper	167
A Petition Remembered	175
Moonlight Memories	188
The Call of the….Couch?	192
The Intervention	203
Oh, What A Name!	206
Great Expectations---Ozark Style	208
The Handshake	210
Rainbow Springs	212
A River's Cries	218
Author's Notes	222

Acknowledgements

Again, I first and foremost wish to thank my wife, Judy, for being there for me always. As a helpmate and best friend, her love encompasses all that is now good in my life. She is the earthly source of my joy and strength.

I wish to thank my neighbor and good friend Mrs. Verna Moss, whose editing has again kept my errors to a minimum. She is a constant inspiration and supporter.

I wish to recognize the influence of the Ozarks themselves. Its people and its principles. Above all, we wish to confess our belief in Jesus Christ as our Lord and Savior, and hope that with this book's publication as well as our endeavors with the Ozark Heritage Project, we truly do Him honor. I thank Him for bringing me to an area so rich with stories and traditions, and ultimately for all the blessings in my life.

About the cover. I took the photos. The barn is in Reynolds County and was built in the 1870's post-Civil War era. Purchased by James and Letha Carter that same century, it hosted a dairy at one time and was home for both work and play for generations of that family. Joyce (Carter) Klingon still visits the structure and reminisces about childhood work and play.

The chair is a cane bottomed chair hand crafted by Alva Bunch, now long gone but a river guide in his youth for Bales Boating. It was designed to be used in a jonboat and was used by another old river guide, Ira Moss, in the 1950's. Alva was my friend and neighbor, Ira along with Waylen Powell entertained me in my youth with stories of the Ozarks. The Ball-Mason jar had the zinc lid and the blue tinting to protect preserves from sunlight. Both the chair and jar were loaned by the Moss Family. Text overlay and cover design are by my nephew Andrew Lough, of Cord Creative.

Picture of Akers Ferry drawn by Hilma Hughes.

Introduction

This collection of short stories represents the effort of several years of writing and several decades of living. A few are born from those innermost thoughts that seep forth in those hours before daylight, others are tales heard and retold; all are based in Ozark tradition and culture.

Several took place during my lifetime with some involving myself and friends firsthand. The meals spoken of were surely eaten; the trails traversed in prose actually trod. We hope to make you laugh with some real characters, but entreat you to not make light of these good people steeped so deeply in tradition. Theirs was a culture that brought not only new life to an area rich in both resource and challenge, but developed and defined a lifestyle still enviable today.

Enjoy these stories, both the real and the imagined, and perhaps say a prayer of thanks for having known some of those mentioned — even if only by word, and for living still in this world He spoke into existence. Who says words do not have power?

Please especially note the organization better defined at book's end, as well as the earlier dedication to a man that truly embodied the spirit of the Ozarks.

A Cargo Predestined

Sharon reached as high as she could, her left foot still on the side of the aluminum johnboat and her right clawing for purchase in the sandy bank.

"I've almost got it" the nineteen year-old announced as she continued to extricate the foreign object from where it was embedded in the rich loam. "Just hold us steady!" The other half of "us" was the fifty-year old uncle and owner of the boat.

"I've got you held. Just don't get hurt." Roy was quite protective of this particular niece, and proud of her participation in this annual stream clean-up. Her mother's bloodline strongly apparent in her lithe six foot tall body, the Osage descendent equally at home with her outdoor surroundings as her ancestors. Cleanliness of the environment is as natural to her as courtesy to her fellow man.

"It's metal on a piece of wood. There's something written" she explains as she regains her seat and Roy proceeds on upstream. "Potts Freight Company. It looks old, ever heard of it?"

Roy thought. He could recall the Potts Hole on Current River; as well as the Potts place, a farm not far below where Barren Fork merges with Sinkin' Creek. A remnant of some old mule and wagon story flickered briefly across his mind. Something his grandfather had talked about in his childhood.

"Potts Freight? Yeah, maybe. I'll study on it."

"Got that harness oiled?" Bill was concerned about yet another day of rain. Though the contract from the state was fairly lucrative, the older of the two brothers knew any business in its infancy had to watch all resources closely. "Watch the dimes; the dollars will take care of themselves!" his father had been fond of saying.

"I did. Almost a quart of linseed, counting the two collars. And before you ask, I used the rags to wipe down all the flat wood surfaces. Thought it might help. Sure made that nameplate shine!" Noah realized his brother and partner was still shaken by the events of the previous week, hoped that reference to the piece of brass they'd engraved and mounted on the one side of their new wagon might cheer him up. They'd placed the gleaming piece of advertising on the right hand side of the white-oak wagon box.

"More people will see it there!" Bill had decided. Noah saw that at last his sibling smiled, despite the happenings from earlier this spring. Only mere days, but now literally a lifetime ago. Dale Jordan's lifetime.

The rain continued to fall. Today they were both on the one wagon. Never completely sure of their cargo until arriving onsite, they believed they would be hauling more timbers from a nearby mill to continue the shoring up of the bridge pillars. They'd been officially working for the state since the past fall, originally hiring on for seventy-five cents a day for them and their pair of mules. Toil and Trouble. Themselves teenagers when their father first purchased and named the mules, they'd since read *Macbeth* and generally believed the fifteen hundred pound mares might well be witches indeed.

The bridge over Current River was just one of the three being built to complete Highway 19 on to Eminence. The brothers had at first pulled construction equipment, their large team getting more out of the Austin Wheeled Scraper than any of the others. Once the majority of the earth had been moved, materials were needed and they purchased an old wagon. Finally they had constructed the cargo box atop the frame built by a West Eminence blacksmith.

Cargos had included rebar and bags of cement as well as locally sawn lumber. At times one brother drove the wagon while the other visited surrounding mills to procure the best of supplies, just one more reason Potts Freight was taking off. The young men were rapidly becoming known for their work ethic and widespread expertise, as well as their giant draft animals. They were considering the order of a second wagon, the blacksmith waiting for the final dimensions and them in search of another team.

Today it turned out they would be hauling pine timbers to be used for reinforcing the pilings. Hollow concrete filled with gravel, the superstructure was starting to form the adjoining arches as fear of an early fall flood was on everyone's mind. The work day had been extended and everyone was being offered a seventh day each week.

The spring of 1923 had not seen a significant rise and some were afraid the fall might very well make up for it.

"You don't mind the company? I'll be some help with that twenty-foot stuff." the younger Noah asked. Two years junior, he was nearly a half-foot taller and unquestionably the physically stronger of the two. The real help he hoped to offer was much more than corporal, and Bill knew it.

"Glad to have you. We can plan that new wagon. I've got some ideas about storage boxes on the sides. Also about adding some more iron loops for tie downs." Bill knew the events of the past week were what were on his brother's mind. Had to admit he was having trouble dealing with what could only be considered the strangest of accidents. It seemed like it had just happened yesterday, instead of a week ago. And then it seemed like ages.

"Haul a what?" Bill had asked.
"A mule. A dead mule. It broke a front leg in harness, had to put it down before it drug the team off the edge of the ridge. They don't want it rotting anywhere near the road. So grab one of my guys and get it out of here."

The "guy" he grabbed was nineteen year-old Dale Jordan. Recently married and with a pregnant wife at home, he was quick to grab a shovel or a rope and assist with whatever task was at hand. All the time wearing a broad smile as he worked up a sweat.

They'd found the dead animal, a small male that had spent years as a "mine mule" because of its smaller stature. Old age and breathing problems had brought him to this job in the fresh air of the lower Ozark Plateau. A worn out heart and a faltering misstep had brought him to this end.

Pulling the wagon off into the ditch and backing his team right below what had only hours before been known as Little Sam, they stopped and got off the wagon. Several of the road crew present were able to drag the deceased animal into the bed of the wagon; rigor not totally set in they folded the back legs up and tucked them inside the walls of the wagon box.

Bill and Dale visited while spending almost an hour hauling the animal far to the other side of the ridge, using a path from which logs had been hauled only the year before. They wanted to make sure that when the rains came whatever was left by the coyotes did not get washed into the clear spring fed stream which they were in the process of bridging.

They backed Toil and Trouble up to the crest of a small hill, put a piece of rope around one of the back legs of Little Sam and pulled forward. Rigor mortis was more complete, the legs now strongly wedged against the oak sides.

"I got it" yelled Dale as he stepped forward. Taking a metal pipe from a storage bin, a tool often referred to as a "cheater pipe" used to tighten chains with a "boomer," he moved to the tail end of the wagon. He inserted the three foot long piece of metal under the uppermost rear leg and began to pry. What happened next was surreal, was seared into Bill's memory he feared forever.

The leg slipped suddenly above the two-inch thick sideboard. What physicists would describe as kinetic energy straightened out the inanimate object, driving the metal shod hoof into the young man's forehead. Dale was dead before hitting the ground.

The next hour passed slowly, painfully so. Bill got on the uphill side and pried up the other leg, enabling his team to easily pull forward and remove the carcass. He then loaded the young man; caringly wrapping him in a tarp they kept to protect certain loads. He kneeled and said a prayer before getting back on the wagon seat and motioning his team forward. Bill noted well the irony as he said the words "Up Toil! Up Trouble!"

The brothers had agreed to empty their own pockets to add to what the foreman was going to give the widow. The young man's body had been moved to a lighter horse drawn carriage, the state employee volunteering to deliver both corpse and news.

That had been a week ago today. Noah was all too aware by the conversation that it weighed heavily on Bill's mind. He talked about everything but; the incident having not been spoken of save for the original telling.

"Ready for a bite of lunch?" the younger man asked. They'd just unloaded their second load and were headed now for the long run to Eminence for nails and other needed materials. They would load this evening and start out early in the morn. The rain had stopped, the sun was hot; and even empty their wagon was of considerable weight.

"Sure. Let's give them a breather before tackling the next hill. We'll rest the team while we eat."

Noah took this as a good sign, as usually they ate while riding. "Let's go down and take a gander at the spring, unhitch the team, the whole works" he suggested.

"Don't want to take that long. We'll chock the wagon and loosen the collars. Grab the water bag and we'll bring them a cool drink, though."

They started past the uppermost rim of the hole that was Round Springs, down the path that would take them to water's edge. They were careful, for even with the present cessation, the rain had made the walk down quite treacherous. Noah had just leaned over to fill the water bag when he heard one of the mules cry out—a cross between a whinny and a bray. Then the rim above them seemed to explode.

The brothers had left the team in a small grove of young elm above the rim, enabling them to rest in shade while allowing Bill to actually tie Trouble to a near sapling. Perhaps a last rumble of thunder or distant flash of lightning from the retreating storm had been the instigator. Perhaps simply erratic fate.

The mules had stepped forward just enough so that when they stepped back the large rock used to scotch the back wheel was now to its side. Once the weight had shifted, momentum drew them rearward and then even the young tree had too little foothold in the moistened ground. Wagon, harness, mules and then tree plummeted over the side. Bill and Noah could only watch in horror as the last vestiges of the disaster sank from sight.

    The rain began again that evening; rained out work for two days. The discharge from the spring increased in volume and darkened in color, taking on the browns and blacks of the local soil. The river rose ten feet. Miraculously the pilings held. No sign was ever seen of either mule or of the wagon itself. Until............

*   Sharon continued to look at the object in her hand. She recognized the metal as brass, realized from high school chemistry that the wood had been preserved by its permanent immersion in water. The flooding earlier this spring had more than likely torn the fragment from beneath the water's surface and deposited it here in the bank where she'd removed it with other articles of trash.*

*   "I do remember something about a wagon and team supposedly being lost in the Spring. Back when they were building the road" Roy was now remembering the story, or at least pieces. Horrible pieces he'd heard spoken of when a child. "That's about all." There was sometimes more to protecting someone than merely the physical.*

Blood Red

I remember the summer of the "pink" Mill. Seems the Park Service boys got their tinting wrong and what was supposed to have been red was at best a "washed out pale deep cerise" as one St. Louis reporter described it. That lasted for a while, but the public outcry caused the park to repaint it long before maintenance required it. Seems the public wanted the Red Mill RED. "The way it had always been!" or so they claimed.

The irony was that the most recent mill at Alley started out white. White with green trim. Or so it was when George McCaskill finally got around to having it painted. When first finished in 1894 it went unpainted for more than a season. And then was painted white. And green. Actually a deep jungle green on the color wheel. A shade of verdigris green. From the *verdigris* process. And they talk about the dangers of lead—try copper acetate! But I digress. Hazard of the profession.

Back to the question at hand. I believe someone asked the color of a mill. Alley Mill, to be precise. Not the original built shortly after the Civil War, but the latest and last. The three story structure that still sits beside the outlet of Alley Springs.

The short answer is red. Blood red. People have been drawn to the clear, clean water of Alley Springs long before it was named. Centuries before machinery harnessed its power to grind corn into meal and wheat into flour, the spring played host to numerous friendly gatherings. It was also frequently the site of conflict.

It was such the winter day of 1543 that Sargento Primera Dario Medina led the small group of Spanish soldiers into its basin, walking up the small stream they'd noticed entering the fork of the river they had chosen only days before. De Soto's force had been decimated by native tribes for dozens of months and hundreds of miles. Diseases for which they'd developed no immunity had been almost as devastating.

Splitting off a small handful of his troops into two additional expeditionary forces, the sergeant major of Basque lineage had been entrusted with one. He and six soldiers had moved westward along the Ozark Plateau and the spring fed streams that crossed it. Weeks after setting out on their own they were tired, short on supplies and needing a place to camp. Here nearing dark they had found it. Walking the alluvial terraces upstream, they now were ready to rest.

Stationing a man on the edge of camp, he sent two more into the woods for firewood. It was one of these two that tried to sound an alarm. Argquebuses were placed on the forked rests, wheel locks cocked and weapons aimed towards an unseen enemy. Arrows flew, half the men fell. Those still on their feet tried to reload as the silent assault continued.

Sergeant Medina was still searching the shadowed recesses of the limestone bluffs before him and the wooded ridge top above for signs of the enemy when the flint-tipped shaft pierced his lung from behind. Stone axes and flint knives finished their work as the more than dozen strong hunting party of the Casqui rushed from concealment. They themselves preparing to camp, they'd heard the approach; prepared the ambush. The almost five-foot long ten pound firearms a liability in close combat, the battle was brief and one sided. The banks that day were red. There's still something to be said for death without gunpowder; it seemed more fitting in such a serene setting.

1767 found the French and Indian War at end, the ink on the Treaty of Paris over three years old. Andre Favreau was not blooded nobility nor a landowner of the bourgeoisie. He had served his country well in battle, even accumulated a few decorations. Still, there was little for which to return home; the military having become his life at a tender age. There was much to explore in this New World.

Coming to the confluence of the Missouri and Mississippi Rivers, he'd visited the trading post established by fellow countryman Pierre Laclede Liguest; leisurely toured the emerging city a year later. In a tent, he'd attended orthodox services with a priest. Had been told of plans for another log structure to serve as a cathedral. Shown where it was to be constructed. Even now he was planning his return to St. Louis in the coming spring, hoping to do so laden with furs and other native treasures.

Favreau was exploring *La Riviere Courante* and its tributaries and surrounding lands that fateful winter afternoon. He'd outfitted his men with .69 caliber Charleville muskets and scabbarded *Boucherons*. Though he carried the same firearm, for a knife he carried a 10-inch Henckels. The German made chef's knife was well suited for skinning as well as cutting through flesh and sinew. He'd acquired it at the Port of Boulogne the evening before embarking for the War. A Hessian mercenary in need of funds made it his at a small café for a fairly steep price. The last article he carried was a .54 caliber British Sea Service pistol. This was literally the spoils of war, taken after a battle in the Ohio Valley over six years before.

Favreau's group of six had been traveling down timbered ridges. The skeletal hardwoods now devoid of their foliage allowed for comprehensive assessment of the terrain. Pierre Beaumont was unofficially recognized as the second in charge. The remaining four turned to him in Favreau's absence. He was an amateur cartographer and had with him a copy of D'Anville's map published in 1752. He was constantly making notes and drawings of the surrounding area. It was during such a time he saw the "hostiles."

Beaumont had been sketching the large spring below him. He'd already mapped the stream coming from it along with the river into which it ran, making notes of the varying kinds of hardwood represented in the bottoms, already having sketched examples of the vast tracts of short-leaf pine. They'd broken camp shortly after daylight and had been traveling for almost three hours.

Favreau directed his men to seek cover behind the surrounding timber. He was under no illusion of being unseen, sure from experience that the dark skinned group in raiment of furs and animal skins had no doubt seen them profiled against the sky. Silently chastising himself for what could now be seen as an obvious tactical mistake, he waited.

The group had been larger than he had first thought, apparent when they came under arrow attack and gunfire from opposite sides. His men acquitted themselves well. Within minutes their superior firepower took its toll. One of his men had received a minor flesh wound from a ricochet, another an arrow in the calf of his leg. They waited for two hours, remaining on guard in case of a subsequent attack. Finally they cautiously approached their attackers.

Favreau did not recognize their apparel. Four had been found dead on the steep slopes from where they'd made their attack. Two more at the shore of the spring pool. He would never know that they were part of a Cherokee hunting party. It was hunger that had driven them to attack, they mistakenly believing the large packs on the backs of the whites to be food stores. They were in fact filled with traps and snaring materials.

What the French adventurer could see was that these people were hungry. They were gaunt, the garments well worn. In the following days they found little game, adding further explanation to the condition and location of the Indians they'd encountered. The scene was all too reminiscent of the years he had hoped to have put behind him. He never could get the image of the blood mixing with the water of the spring from his head. He did return to St. Louis that next spring and made a living of leading forages into surrounding forests and ensuring the security and safety of the logging teams. His work was instrumental to the erection of the first St. Louis cathedral. He was buried in 1775 on the eve of America's revolution. I understand from an associate his great-nephew used the Henckels to defend himself from a burglar in 1804. Certainly not the last time kitchen cutlery was involved in a violent crime.

    Hu lah tse stood apart from his warriors; alone in his own thoughts. His naming ceremony only a few short seasons behind him, War Eagle had always believed battle to be in his future. The clash with the Caddo hunting party was inevitable, they being a long running enemy of the Osage. Territorial disputes along with conflicts over resources led to many such battles. Had led to this morning's.

    The Osage had spotted the small herd of elk the day before. They had hoped to take at least several, the hides and bones almost as important as the meat. They were set for the kill this morning when suddenly one of the cows broke into a run, the flowing blood showing easily against the whitish rump that had given them the Shawnee name wapiti. The competing tribe had not only spoiled the hunt by firing on them, but their pursuit ran them headlong into War Eagle.

The skirmish was brief. Two Osage died, three of the Caddos before they withdrew. The female elk had rejoined the herd as it fled, its present health status unsure. Gone almost three weeks, the young Osage leader had hoped to return with much needed supplies for his tribe. It was in this frustrated state of mind that he resumed his trek homeward.

Bill and Velma Coops had heard of this spring. Had planned to camp here, perhaps even build a cabin from the surrounding pine. Warned of hostiles, they'd fled the urban jungle that was becoming St. Louis. Despite their recent achievement of statehood, Missouri's largest city was still struggling economically. The Panic of 1819 had wiped out the young couple, they among the many caught up in land speculation through local banks. Bill still recalled stories that had filtered back from Lewis and Clark's now two decade old expedition. Fur. Mineral deposits. Timber. Enticed by such tales of treasure, they had decided the adventure was worth the risk. They'd sold their home, bought the two oxen and cart and headed south.

War Eagle was not proud of the afternoon's events. In some ways they had been worse than the morning's. They had supplies. Some metal tools and more of what could only be described as trinkets. Some heavy coats and living meat and hides that could be driven back to their summer grounds. Still, Hu la tse had never enjoyed making war on women. Even one with so valiant a defender as the man had proven to be. The evening's wind finally drove her screams from his mind.

The War of Northern Invasion had been over for six years. The Secret Order of the Sons of Liberty was in its third. The state census of last year reflected the slow recovery of their county of Shannon. Their home. Still not back in pre-War production levels in corn or cattle, much of the most recent activity was on lands being stolen from friends and relations.

Farms and homesteads that had belonged to families that had been driven from the state were being sold for back taxes to immigrants that their own government was inviting into the state. Land cleared and homes built by hard labor and at times great risk being sold for pennies on the dollar to people whom had been part of the Invasion. Or worse, had not even worn a uniform and only now sought to reap that for which others had died.

Well, not tonight. Not this!

The "this" of which the group was concerned was the mill at what people were calling Alley Springs. In just the past few years the small community had got a post office and it was named after the family with the largest farm—Alley. It was officially Alley Post Office.

The grist mill was doing a good business. Too good of business, at least so the Sons believed, considering that the owners barely spoke English—not being long from the Deutschland. They'd purchased the spring and several hundred acres from a St. Louis bank that had foreclosed on the property in the midst of the War. Northern interests had stolen the government and they and their friends were making the most of it.

Not everyone was sympathetic with their cause, many wishing that order would be restored and the unpleasantness finally stopped. Hence the presence of weapons. Corn knives. Daggers. Axes and hatchets. The family operating the business was known to work late Saturday nights to clean and repair machinery for the following work week. What the self-declared patriots had not known was that the children would be helping and that the women had brought them all supper.

All in all nine bodies were thrown into the pool that evening. Due to the form of slaughter, the pool that night was almost black it was so blood stained. The full moon, that allowed the killers to operate without lantern or torch, had cast an eerie reflection upon the sides of the wooden structure. Faded pine boards took on a pale crimson hue, as did the limestone bluffs. That I remember as a quite beautiful evening; a most wondrous sight. That is why I will always think of Alley Mill, even Alley Springs and its setting, as Blood Red. But, then again, why ask me? I'm neither architect nor stylist; designer or artist. I'm merely a Death Haint!

The Table

    She still remembered the day he brought the wood home. A cherry tree had blown over in the adjoining field of a neighbor and Paul had been recruited to cut the massive tree off the fence, the more than three foot circumference that had developed over at least a century and a half of struggling and thriving in the Ozark climate far greater than the farmer's small chainsaw could handle. Although more than a decade had passed since he cut timber for a living, Paul yet kept the Stihl 66 saw of his own sharp and ready to go. The tree had taken two trips with his trailer, even the limbs creating four and six foot logs well over twelve inches in diameter.

    The logs had lain there in the edge of the pasture all summer and then had been hauled to a friend that owned a small portable mill, one of the band saws built on its own trailer. This one was actually pushed along the rails of the trailer, reducing the cost of both purchase and operation. An agreement had been reached to saw the logs into lumber, the service traded for being that Paul wire a new home for the recently married son of the mill's owner. The call came for the work to finally be done on a crisp December morning and the first two pickup loads were designated as Christmas presents. Both one and two-inch boards were sawn, the upper part of the trunk providing knot-free lumber more than sixteen inches in width. Stripped and stacked in the back of a shed, the lumber then lay there for two years, Jenny adhering to the "one inch per year" requirement of air-drying hardwood.

Almost three years to the day from the spring storm that had fell the monstrous cherry; Jenny began her first project with the much-considered lumber. She'd reviewed woodworking magazines, taken measurements in antique stores, and even sketched an item or two during museum visits. What was begun in April was finally concluded in early June, the target date of a fifth anniversary having been successfully met. When Paul returned from his day at the office; gleaming with a fresh coat of varnish and sharing a floor position somewhat to the south of the fireplace and right in front of the east facing picture window, sat a new dining room table complete with four Quaker style chairs. Two China place settings, from an eight person set purchased years before while attending Oklahoma Christian College and considering life as viewed peering into the future as opposed to reflecting upon a past, graced each end. A wooden vase with fresh cut flowers sat in between, leaving the majority of the reddish brown tabletop to be seen.

"That's beautiful; just like the builder!" Paul could always be counted on for some compliment, often more than Jenny believed she deserved. These words were greatly appreciated, as was the look on his face. It shone, as did the table. The now setting sun reflected off them both. The one, painstakingly smoothed by hand; the other rough and lined, but never hardened.

Over the years the table saw much activity, most serene and pleasant; all heartfelt and encased in love. Here the two shared morning breakfasts and evening meals. After a stillborn birth, the other two chairs were eventually filled by first a daughter and then a healthy son. In the interim, other young couples had been invited to eat and share a card game of pitch or thoughtful study of the Bible. Saturdays too rainy to go afield or work at the ever present chores of a small farm tended only after a forty-hour career obligation was fulfilled, Paul was often joined by one of the neighbors for a game of chess or checkers --- the "field of battle" always the selection of the guest and never easily deciphered by the opponent's occupation. His most challenging chess matches were the result of mental jousting between himself and a local barber whom had never completed the sixth grade but found life as a small town hair-cutter left a lot of time to read. A circuit judge who dropped in when business brought him through the district much preferred checkers, perhaps the lesser intensity of their game gave them increased opportunity to visit.

During the day, the table served as platform for sewing projects and even the occasional quilting bee. A daughter's first recital dress took form on the by then worn surfaces of cherry, as did a young man's conversion from three to the very much more "adult" four button shirts. Late winter evenings Paul would sit facing the fireplace and make notes for a sermon to be soon delivered, many of their Sundays now spent as he volunteered his services for vacationing preachers or to small congregations that found themselves unable to afford a minister. Sunrises, particularly within those months of the calendar when such astrological events came early, found Paul reading from some selection of his limited but valued library. Jenny was setting the table often as he first devoured advice and direction from Aurelius' *Mediations,* irony from Guy de Maupassant's *Short Stories,* a sense of justice from Hugo's *Les Miserables* and Dostoevsky' *Crime and Punishment,* or the simplistic beauty of life found in the pages of Whitman's *Leaves of Grass.*

  Birthday gifts were unwrapped and the accompanying celebratory cakes eaten from this table. Handmade Christmas gifts often finished and then wrapped on the table, Christmas cards addressed and signed, birthday greetings stamped and prepared for mailing. A slip in the mud and the quickness of an angered sow, the tearing of flesh and the nicking of an artery; an older uncle's leg was actually amputated on that very table. Admittedly, although all that remained of that horrid evening was a slight scratch where a knife had gone through three layers of handmade quilts and a canvas tarp, the visual picture of the evening made dining on the porch preferable for the next couple of evenings and for a decade plates or mats were strategically placed to obscure the imperfection until it finally became somewhat lost in subsequent attacks on the hardwood surface.

  Good times come and go, markets rise and fall, and careers take sudden turns. Though only a mid-level state employee, Paul witnessed one too many examples of graft and bureaucratic waste; the end to this storyline was written long ago and has been repeated for centuries. Contrary to fairy tales and sitcom television scripts, nice guys do not always prevail in the end. Not, at least, at the end of every battle. A few names were changed, new conduits of exploitation explored, taxpayers continued to be scammed and Paul found himself out of work and virtually unemployable.

The table became a "war room" where losses were counted and attrition estimated. Their few head of cattle were first to be sold off, then the tractor he'd been so proud to finally purchase. Almost a year went by. Jenny had substitute taught and Paul had got a job bucking logs for a small logging outfit operating two hours away. Long days he slept in the bed of his truck and saved the gas money by skipping the drive home. His fishing boat was long since gone, as were the majority of his guns.

It was on one of those days that Jenny received notice from the bank. Their years of faithful payments a consideration, the awarded moratorium on principle was over and they were now the dreaded ninety days past due. Foreclosure was more than a possibility; it was imminent. A remembered complement and inquiry was retrieved from days gone by and a phone call later an offer was indeed proffered. The next day the mortgage was caught up, there was a "safety net" in the bank, and the furniture re-arranged. Somewhat.

As Paul parked his pickup that evening, the usual jubilation of his arrival was tempered with trepidation. He had loved the cherry furniture as much as she, had often commented on the history it had seen, on the building of a nation that had taken place around the tree itself. The fact that she had sawn it out, sanded and assembled it with her own hands made it mean that much more to the both of them. Even their children bragged about it when with their visiting friends. No interior planning could cover the void. The handmade pieces had been too large, too noticeable. The form and function that made it so conspicuous, along with the boards depicting over a century of growth within their grain, combined to make the table and chairs worth the equivalent of several months' salary.

She could feel her heart in her throat as he opened the door. Her eyes glanced guiltily towards the now vacant space of floor. "I had to sell ……. the mortgage is caught up ……. a little's left over for emergencies…" she struggled to explain.

He hushed her with a kiss as he took her in his arms. As so often at the end of a serious discussion or when encountering a problem, he twirled her around and went through his best imitation of a waltz. With a true understanding of what indeed was valuable, he smiled as he told her, "Look, honey! Now we finally have room to dance."

The Picture

The last remnants of a waning sun accented the white hairs on his face. He sat quietly, settled against the back of the bench as if gathering the last vestiges of warmth in defense of the chill that would come with dark. We'd met on the sidewalk only moments ago, nodding polite hellos as we passed. It was then I'd noticed the teddy bears in his left arm. One dressed in patriotic red, white and blue. The other in miniature versions of the desert camouflage that had been clothing our armed forces for the past two and a half decades. Around the gentleman's neck hung a small framed camera. A Minolta. We photographers notice such things.

More accurately, I'm a photo journalist. Emphasis on journalist, as my photographic skills are at best advanced novice. Photos accompany the stories I sell; the words are what I'm paid for. This coming year, I hope to change that. To that end I recently purchased what many consider the lowest end of a semi-professional camera; others a mid-range amateur's. This afternoon was its first outing. A decent Nikon full frame box with a fairly nice zoom lens going out to 300mm. Purchased with wildlife in mind, today I hoped to capture humans.

I wanted pictures that spoke for themselves. That captured some feeling; perhaps some inner conflict. That gave the viewer a glimpse into some other aspect of life. A bit enough to generate interest, but leaving room for suspense and speculation. Great pictures tell a story. Great stories hold some mystery. I wished for pictures that were a door opened just wide enough to invite inquisitive entry.

The sun was setting and light, or the lack thereof, was about to become my enemy. I framed the shot, using a majestic pin oak in the background for a border. The light still was good on the two stuffed animals, the palest one somewhat resembling a small child. Tightening the zoom revealed the wrinkles in a weathered face. The flag lapel pin. A final expansion of the shot and a check of the f stop and I was ready. Then he turned. My finger stopped.

It wasn't so much that I had wanted the portrait in profile as the expression on his face. It silently screamed. No, that sounds too frantic. It commanded "Do not." Do not take my picture. Do not invade my space. Do not intrude upon my privacy. I lowered my camera.

I nodded my resignation, and quietly sought a different pathway to take my leave. It has been said that "Civilization is the progress toward a society of privacy." I had vowed long ago to not let any profession come before my humanity; I could not put a potential dollar ahead of common courtesy and what I believed a required display of respect.

I turned once and looked back. He sat staring at what now was an autumn dusk. I wondered if indeed he was ex-military. He had the bearing. Were the stuffed animals all that remained of a lost childhood? A fallen son that had followed in a father's footsteps and not been allowed to return home? An act of remembrance of a loved one; perhaps the manifestation of defiance in a nation seemingly unaware of those giving "that last full measure of devotion?" I walked on; fully aware I would now never know. It would have been a great shot.

Grandpa's New Book

At seventy-three my grandfather was in fine physical condition; especially for a man who spent the first half of his life with a cigarette constantly in hand. He had always been a man of almost insatiable intellect, scouring more than two dozen periodicals monthly for anything he might find of interest. Literary waters in which he fished ranged from the building of hot rods to the latest in instructional intervention for the learning disabled. His personal library contained the works of Hugo, Dickinson, and Saint-Exupery alongside those of L'Amour, Cantor and Hall. It was only in the past few years they'd been joined by a leather bound copy of the King James Bible.

Perhaps a close-call with cancer, though WWII had made death an acquaintance years before. Maybe wisdom of a nature not found in books. Regardless of the reasons, Grandpa had been eagerly in pursuit of all things spiritual for some time. He attended Gospel Meetings and Revivals. He studied the word as commissioned by that Scottish heir to the throne some four centuries ago. He strove to somehow apply not only the teachings of Jesus and His apostles to his life, but to immerse himself in the lifestyle of that time to the degree possible. He ate a Middle-eastern diet as much as Midwest grocery stores allowed. He traded in his Stanley thermos for a genuine goatskin water bag; began hiking our Ozark woods in leather sandals.

All of this I took in stride; even glad that however many years on this earth he was still allotted, his next life was secured. I perhaps worried a bit about the possibility of snakebites given the new footwear or even gastric problems via the water storage. When I found him prone on the ground, head against the soil and covered in large part by leaves, I did wonder. Two days later with similar observations, I had to ask.

"Son, I've heard whippoorwills, geese, the celebrative songs of meadowlarks well fed and the cries of their babies when being swallowed by snakes. I've heard the explosive rustle of quail being flushed, the tornadic sound of turkeys leaving a roost at night, the howl of coyotes surrounding a kill, the yelp of their pups at play; the call of turkey hens and the gobble of their male suitors. I've listened to the hoots of great horned owls, even heard their shriek as they fell upon a rabbit and the victim's screams as it was lifted into the sky."

I knew my grandfather to have been quite the outdoorsmen, and was not surprised that the same ears that discriminate between the French horn's contributions in Tchaikovsky's *Fourth Symphony* and Stravinsky's *Firebird Suite* would be so attuned to the sounds of our forests. He continued.

"I've heard the warning of a rattlesnake from within striking range, the grunt of a feral boar cornered by my hounds, the growl of a bobcat trying to share a tree stand, the laughter like sound of a raccoon wetting his food creek side. I've listened to the bleats of deer, the crashing of their antlers in combat. Even the whinny of those so-called wild horses running amok in our parks. Last year was privy to the bugling of elk right here where they'd been killed out a century and a half ago. And that's just here in Missouri. You take my travels in Europe, my hunting in Alaska, my fishing in the Gulf and parts south, until a month ago I'd heard about every creature God had made. Then I read it."

Now here was a man whom had traversed parts of the Asian and African continents, let alone read Corbett's *Man Eaters of Kumaon* and Hemingway's *Death in the Afternoon* and *The Green Hills of Africa*. It was difficult to imagine what he could have read that would be so surprising. I'd learned years before that it was not only considered by him to be rude to interrupt, but that such a move only prolonged the delay until his presentation would continue. I remained curious, but quiet.

"I know species vary from land mass to land mass, but there is still a familial continuity. It's not like I was chasing some mythical beast such as a unicorn. The wisest man ever to walk this planet identified this occurrence. I wanted to experience it for myself. Hence the humble posture. For when you think about it, it may have been as much about spiritual attitude as physical alignment to hear it. And what more unassuming speaker? It would be as if the Earth itself was speaking."

My grandfather had been a fighter pilot in war, a petroleum engineer in peace. A driver of cars and motorcycles in races. He spoke five languages. Albeit kindly, he considered me his intellectual inferior. At moments such as these, I hated to offer support for his hypothesis. Still, his silence invited a response.

"I'm lost. What is it you are hoping to experience? Obviously some kind of animal sound, I expect."

"Animal sound?" He sounded almost indignant. "I believe it much greater than just a sound. Solomon called it a voice."

I was still lost; adrift in fact and speculation. I remained silent. Grandpa did not.

"You read the Bible, right? I mean, you do preach and all? Song of Solomon 2:12? It's right there."

I left, evening was approaching and I had chores to do. Grandpa was headed to the woods behind his house. Later that evening, curiosity again became my captain and I gathered the NIV Study Bible from my desk. A few flips of the pages revealed the following:

"Flowers appear on the earth; the season of singing has come, the cooing of doves is heard in our land."

Nothing extreme. My Grandpa and I have dove hunted together. Have listened to them in the evenings as they fed over fields of sunflowers in the summer. I admit I pretty much put the issue aside.

Until. A few nights later my grandmother called, it was an hour past dark and Grandpa had not returned to the house. Not extremely rare, but not common either. I was almost an hour's drive myself, so suggested she call some neighbors. When I got there, Grandpa was in his recliner looking longingly out his living room window. A neighbor just up the road had found him a little ways up a side hollow. He'd not fallen, as he assured everyone. He was lying in a bed of barely protruding bluebells near the bottom of a wet weather creek. When he tried to get up, he had "a hitch in his get-along" and was unable to rise. Pressure on his chest made his calls for help inaudible.

"What now, Grandpa?" I asked with worry obvious in my voice. "Dove cooing?"

"Dove cooing? What are you talking about?"

"The scripture. Song of Solomon 2:12. Doves cooing."

His look reminded me that his belief in my intellectual shortcomings was still there. "Son, grab that Bible from the table."

There it sat. The blackened leather cover just beginning to show signs of wear. Gold embellished *King James Version* right on the spine. A few careful turns of the page revealed the answer to the several week old mystery. It practically leapt off the page.

"The flowers appear on the earth; the time of the singing of birds is come

and the voice of the turtle is heard in our land."

I finished reading. I lay the Bible back on the table. The "earth itself" speaking. A "humble spirit" needed for the hearing. The lying prostrate on the ground. All these now made sense.

Grandpa's search to hear what perhaps had never been heard. The misunderstanding evident; as was the need for me to purchase my grandfather a newer translation of His Word.

The Bucket List

I knew that my uncle I was about to visit was up in years, "short of tooth" they used to say; but I was not nearly prepared for what greeted me when I pulled my truck into his driveway. He was seated on his porch, pencil and paper in hand; a glass of tea by his side.

"What are you up to?" I asked, unaccustomed to him not being at work this time of the day. After all, it was past lunch and a long time until the spring day turned to dusk.

"Making my bucket list" he replied. "Thought it about time."

I was dumbstruck. Just a few weeks ago he'd been splitting wood like a teenager. I wondered if I'd heard him correctly. "You're what?" I inquired further.

"My bucket list. Just this morning I found myself almost falling in my garden, both hands clutched to my chest. Knew then that it was time. So I'm makin' 'er right now. No more time left to put it off."

Trying to keep an onslaught of fear and sadness at bay, I continued. "This seems kind of sudden," I suggested. "Are you sure?"

"Well, it's been coming longer than I like to let on. I was getting a drink the other morning, waiting for the sun to crest the ridge and knock a bit of cool from my old bones, when it hit me. Things wear out. The old must be set aside, the new embraced. Sometimes a few parts might be salvaged; other times its best to just accept that it's over and what was once a precious vessel should now be thrown in a ditch to help slow down erosion. I'm sure your aunt won't let me do that, though." He smiled.

I knew my uncle to be a pragmatist who, though deeply compassionate, shunned most public displays of sentiment. Still, this was going some. "Is it your heart?" I was almost afraid to hear the answer.

"Is what my heart?" he looked puzzled. "Not sure what you mean."

I swallowed hard. "What you're dying from. Is it your heart?"

"I ain't dying! Who said anything about dying?" he was now looking perturbed.

"The bucket list you're sitting there making. Clutching your chest in the garden this morning and nearly falling. The empty vessel you're about to throw away." I was talking rapidly, wondering if I was being understood.

"Before I get to the feed store, I want to make sure I know what I need. When I drew that water the other morning and more spilled back into the well than I was getting to drink; despite that being the well bucket that we bought fifty years ago---I should have replaced it then. But I didn't. Kind of slipped my mind, especially since we have water piped throughout the house. When I nearly fell this morning, having gathered up those loose rocks and nothing to be done but bundling them in my arms against me and trying so hard not to drop a single one I almost fell---you don't have to hit me over the head! I needed some new buckets. So I'm making a list."

I joined him in a glass of cold tea while he finished up. Seems galvanized tin "captures the flavor" of well water best, and "those heavy rubber buckets" are the most durable to carry rocks from the garden. Metal one gallon ones are best for giving away tomatoes and cucumbers in the summer. It's a pretty good list.

The Blizzard Brunch

As wind driven snow blanketed the table and pan of fish, numbing hands clawed at the chores of scaling and de-finning the extremely large suckers. Even as scales and skin were quickly coated with an impenetrable coating of ice, smiles adorned the faces of the three outdoorsmen as they tried to recall if they had ever cleaned fish in more adverse conditions.

"You ever see the like?" Calvin inquired of his father while once again having to submerge the two-pound hog sucker he was holding in order to temporarily loosen the ice and remove what scales he could in the brief interim the frigid environment afforded. As his sixty-six year old father and patriarch of the family prepared to respond, Calvin realized he'd removed the scales from less than one-half of one side of the fish and the aluminum scaling tool could once more no longer penetrate the frozen exterior of the intended meal.

As his son again plunged the frozen fish carcass he was holding under the stream of the garden hose, Phil began his response. "Son, do you mean the fact that we're standing here cleaning fish and I can barely see across the table for the buckets of snow falling, or that despite the fact I bought the best brass nozzle around, and regardless of my always hanging it on a hook on this wooden cleaning table, I once more am subjected to the constant, un-controlled and overwhelming flow of water from a nozzle-less garden hose?" Winds approaching thirty miles an hour and the horizontal passage of the immense volume of snowflakes in the air still did not completely hide the look of incredulity on the son's face.

"I should have thrown that thing over the hill the first time you left it hanging out here" the forty-three year old co-owner of Blazer Boats muttered more to himself than to his father. Now working on the second side of what half-covered with snow was coming to resemble some arctic leviathan, he turned to the third member of the party. "Every time he turned that thing on, we were soaked with its high pressure blast. Knives were washed from the table, fish washed to the ground, and Eric, did I mention—we were always soaked. That'd be great in this outdoors freezer we're in right now!"

"Eric," the more senior partner in Blazer Boats now also addressed the retired educator turned writer, "did you ever see such a hard-headed rascal?" Phil continued to note that somehow he'd "raised a blockhead" too stubborn to recognize technological advances, such as the now absent brass attachment had offered, and impervious to great gifts, both of wisdom and things material, had "probably already thrown it over the hill as if the things we needed in life would just reappear in spring with the return of robins and redbuds!"

Happy the question of Calvin's stubbornness had been of a rhetorical nature and he'd not had to address it or the fact that he'd been asked virtually the exact same question by other members of the family about the father and several uncles, Eric thought back to how their present predicament had begun. Invited to their friend's river cabin the night before, Eric and his wife joined three generations of the Moss family to bring in the New Year. Supper had consisted of a variety of smoked meats and side dishes, with the entertainment planned the Disney movie *Snowball Express.* With a daughter-in-law expressing a taste for fried suckers, a gigging trip had been hurriedly put together. Shortly after the majority of the smoked meats were consumed, father, son and teen-age granddaughters were accompanied by the writer on a Current River sojourn to gather the winter-hardened bottom feeders.

      Writer and elder Moss visited and ran the boat while the son and patriarch's granddaughters proceeded to gather several more than two dozen. The current cold snap concentrated fish in the deeper holes, where the increased clarity of the water combined with the more lethargic movement of the suckers to make successful harvesting of the larger specimens well within the ability of not only the long-seasoned veteran but the young Molly as well. Arriving back at the cabin about time to start the movie, a decision was made to just gut the fish and put them in water in an outside refrigerator until morning. There was both a feeling of relief at having severely reduced the task at hand and a sense of foreboding among the older members of the party who had terrible recollections of the few times they'd postponed such chores in the past. Nevertheless, entrails removed, fish carcasses were soon placed in a non-running refrigerator and stored away until morning.

The comedic actions of Dean Jones and Harry Morgan were enjoyed, final cookies eaten and last cup of hot chocolate swallowed, midnight celebrated—more sleepily by some than by others—and the writer and wife returned to their home. The Moss's settled down for the night, agreement having been reached that they would gather at around nine later that morning and begin the New Year with a breakfast of scrambled eggs, biscuits and gravy and as a main entrée—fried fish! Such was the plan.

What the plan did not take into consideration was the Gulf Stream un-expectantly dropping southward nearly two hundred miles and the temperatures hitting single digits by daylight. Enough moisture had come up the Mississippi Basin to produce a blizzard. A blizzard that arrived at the refurbished fish camp about fifteen minutes after nine. Just enough time for the three males of the previous night's agreement to have opened the icebox and realized they were looking at sucker-sicles!

Calvin retrieved the water hose from where it had been placed inside the cabin, their one good decision; while Phil set up the table and Eric began carrying the fish. Though moments before still warm, the hose was nearly frozen as the ice cold water began flowing through it. The table sat askew on the surface of the frozen yard, there being no hope of digging out divots to make it level. It took two sets of hands to separate the fish, two grown men pulling in opposite directions while the third controlled the water.

"Who'd have thought there'd be this much blood left after we gutted them?" inquired Phil, he being given the job of cutting off heads and fins after Eric had scaled them.

"Dad, you've cut your hand!" exclaimed Calvin. "It's you who's bleeding."

"Nonsense" Phi countered as he ran more water over the now headless yellow sucker in his hand.

"Tell him, Eric. Maybe he'll believe you!"

Eric was having his own struggles. Trying to get another fish ready for decapitation, he'd pushed through to complete a whole side without re-wetting the fish. The thin metal fish scaler had broken in the strain, with the result being the ragged edge tearing itself into the numbed hand attempting to keep the fish on what was basically a sheet of ice on four legs.

"Yeah, what he said" was his somewhat weak offering. "Might even have scratched my own hand, Phil. Easy to do in this cold."

Calvin just shook his head. The driving wind and what now were more icy pellets than snowy flakes made opening his eyes much beyond a squint extremely difficult; still he was quite sure what he saw before him was the white of bone on one of his father's fingers and a slice of skin and flesh literally flapping as Eric clumsily ran the now handle-less scaler down the sides of the fish.

"Guys, you think maybe we should quit? Surely we have enough cleaned for now?" Calvin asked, believing an appeal to the urgency of eating might carry more weight than another plea for their health. "We've got 'taters, biscuits, gravy and stuff. Plenty to feed us and have leftovers for lunch."

Phil and Eric still remembered well the postponement from the night before and were reticent to tempt fate once more.

"Been there, done that" responded Phil, he now trying to utilize a hatchet to cut through frozen flesh and bone. Fears of self-amputation flashed into the mind of Calvin as he watched. As he believed his anxiety could get no worse; Eric was getting the toolbox from his truck. After a bit of rummaging around, he returned with a hammer, some nails and a chainsaw.

The next effort was not as bad as he'd first imagined. Eric used the hammer and nails to secure the fish to the table, and then the bar and chain, sans engine, to scrape the scales from the fish. Meanwhile Phil operated the hatchet with renewed vim and vigor. Once one side was so de-scaled, the fish had to be turned over. Calvin continued to wet the menagerie of tools, food and hands and was seconds from conceding things were on the upswing when it came time to turn the fish, to scale the other side.

First, the nails had to be removed. Between the gore from the hatcheted beheading and the ice pellets building up on everything (and yes—everything does include the backs of necks and ears, the backs of hands and somehow even the corners of eyes), the heads of the nails were difficult to locate. Once found, their extrication proved even more trying.

The groove between the claws was filled and Calvin had to spray the hammer repeatedly, all the while he awaited some comment from his father about that discarded nozzle. Then once the nail head was secured above the arc of metal, little leverage could be attained to actually pull the nails. What moments before had appeared to be frozen flesh became a mass of pulp as pressure was applied. This was a fairly frictionless substance, causing the tool to slip and suddenly a knuckle to be impaled on the still well embedded nail. Now even Phil had to concede that it was indeed human blood being faithfully washed away by Calvin's still steady hand. Eric just stared; one could only wonder if the stoic expression was in recognition of his now damaged appendage or at the ever present prospect of having to scale the other side of the fastly secured fish.

The wind was coming in gusts; visibility was decreasing by the minute. The women inside had been spared watching all this, the men taking refuge behind the blind side of the house. It will never be known if a single window allowing the watchful eyes of what many consider the more intelligent of the species may have prevented at least some of the morning's casualties. None the less, even Calvin was having trouble seeing the events that were continuing to transpire.

Phil used the bar, after removing the chain, to literally rip Eric loose. Then, he used the same bar to pry up the fish. A judicious use of the jagged edge of the scaler broken what seemed days ago cleaned the other side. Throughout all this, the one area of relief was the fish cooker that had been burning for over two hours. Nestled behind a rack of wood and now further protected by a couple of strategically placed pieces of cardboard, it had offered a bit of reprieve from what were surely sub-zero wind chill temperatures. All three now huddled over the propane flame, warming themselves and mutually speculating on how soon the oil would be at the requisite 350 degrees.

The now ice-covered table became the work station for scoring and mealing the almost two dozen fish (mercifully several could no longer be seen and would be discovered by barn cats in the days following the now historic breakfast). Pocket knives were withdrawn from pockets, not easily mind you as unfortunately they were in jeans beneath insulated coveralls and raincoats (Calvin's water distribution without the nozzle was not nearly as accurate as he liked to believe). Calvin resumed garden hose duties and Eric and Phil continued to make the cuts every one-quarter inch or so and from the skin down to the backbone. The flesh being partly frozen actually made this job easier; the hands manipulating the knives being partially frozen negated any such advantage. Visibility was near zero; all feeling lost in hands and fingers. Human skin was as without the sense of touch as were that of the soon to be meals.

It was during the mealing stage that the real cost of the cuisine started to be seen.

"Most of these fish are huge" remarked Phil.

"I know, Dad" replied Calvin, checking the amount of meal on each piece prior to placing it in the grease. "Is that why you filleted this one?" This last enquiry came as a piece of cornmeal covered flesh half the size of a playing card and not much thicker was entering the cooking pot.

The meal was finally eaten. The eggs were scrambled as the last of the fish were cooked; biscuits brought from a warming oven and gravy re-heated with the addition of a half a cup of milk.

Eric had indeed lost a significant slab of flesh from his one hand, as well as the use of one digit. Actually the joint of one digit; doctors were fairly sure that he'd regain the use of the joints below the wounded knuckle. With therapy. The hand needed only time. The majority of the cuts from scoring were superficial, nary a stitch and only a few butterfly bandages.

Phil required numerous stitches. The one cut first noticed by his son during the early beheadings took twenty-seven by itself; others from later in the processing took a dozen more. His worst injuries were from cooking. In retrospect, when returning from a short hiatus inside to warm up, he should have worn more than house slippers (in his defense—they were fleece lined). Only one of his burns required skin grafts; all four the daily changing of bandages.

Calvin did not come away unscathed. Since during much of the ordeal he was witnessing things too horrible to remember, let alone recount (he was actually considering taking that 'small fillet' from the cooker to taste test when the raw patch on Eric's hand brought realization); he believed he'd been subconsciously suppressing the images. Turns out, due to his stance at the head of the work table, blowing ice crystals had actually scarred both of his corneas. Surgery on the first had not gone well; the operation on the second was still on hold.

The Gift

"What was the best gift you ever gave?" Steve asked as he laid a small stick of sycamore on the fire. Now little more than a bed of coals and very much in need of the added fuel, the small stack of axe cut logs had been a silent witness to the ongoing conversation between the four old friends. Gigging had been productive here at the end of the season, and the oil was cooling in the cast-iron Dutch oven now that the meal was finished. All the onion and hushpuppies were gone, a few cooked fillets and a handful of potatoes were wrapped in foil and resting on the back seat of the truck. The boat had been loaded and readied for the trip home.

Ben was first to respond. Already they'd covered "most expensive", "most difficult to find" and "least appreciated." The topic of gifts had followed recollections of best holiday meals, furthest distance traveled under adverse conditions (265 miles in a snowstorm for Valentine's Day made Curtis the winner on that one) and failed romances that had been initiated or inspired during the holiday season.

The belly pan valves were frozen once again, and he was momentarily stumped as how to thaw them out. Not wanting to waste the same hour that yesterday morning had cost him prior to heading to the bulk plant, then because of a leaking fuel line. Any kind of flame was certainly out of the question, given the cargo about to be loaded and distributed. The thermometer had read 27 degrees Fahrenheit when he'd left the house, and he could not afford to start loading if there was any doubt about any of the five compartments not being fully closed. About to take refuge in a cup of hot coffee, the idea "poured forth." Literally. A few minutes later, secure in the knowledge that the gate valves at the bottom of each of the compartments were indeed closed and would remain so until the requisite levers were pulled, the flow from four separate three-inch hoses dumped distinctly different fuels into their own storage units. Concentrating on watching each compartment fill to its individual marker kept him from noting the film of petroleum collecting in his airways, a film that served as both irritant and limiter to his now challenged breathing. So far during the past week and the start of this one not one drop had overflowed. Off and on road diesel, no lead and premium gasoline; all had been shut off in time for nozzles to be removed and hatches closed with little mess. The headaches did not come until the third day, his doctor's supposition that his diminished lungs weren't getting enough oxygen upstairs. Much the same reason his arms ached from fighting the ten tons of bed and cargo without the assistance of power steering; a new hydraulic pump not currently in the budget.

   Taking a curving hill, he quickly downshifted to the high side of fourth, taking advantage of the "working five's" peculiarity that this gear change was in fact only half a speed down and required no decrease in engine rpm, as would the later split-shifting of the two-

speed axle. The gas-powered 366 had little torque at lower rpm's, just another reason they had been discontinued more than two decades earlier. Feeling the liquid load surge, he was forced to slow his ascent as the curve became more sharp. Now the race to find a gear that would continue both his momentum and his needed engine speed and hopefully prevent the taking the curve in only second gear and topping the hill at a snail's pace, placing him even further behind before even his first stop.

"I bought my brother-in-law a used boat. He had recently changed jobs, his two kids had moved away and he was in danger of immersing himself in his work. My sister had mentioned several times how much the two enjoyed fishing together. They were now a long ways from the river they'd trout-fished for years, and the waters available pretty much required some sort of vessel. I had a pretty good used outboard, so I purchased a used boat and trailer and Christmas morning they all were his." Ben omitted a few of the details. He had in fact given the brother-in-law a small tackle box with a selection of lures. In the last compartment, down from some silver Cordell Spots and across from a grey and black Zara Spook, were the keys to the remote start and a note directing him outside to the driveway where the boat had been sneaked in late the night before.

"When later that spring" Ben went on, "my sister told me of the late afternoons and early evenings they'd already enjoyed on a nearby lake and even occasionally on the mighty Missouri River; well, I knew I'd done a good thing."

He'd dreaded the morning, physically losing sleep because of his anxiety. It was not just the forecasted cold (the thermometer had indeed read in the teens when he left the house), but the fear of making a mistake coupled with the constant battling of the machine in which was placed his friend's financial future as well as his own physical survival. The driver's side shock absorber was in a storage bin behind him, the king pins in the front end noticeably worn as could be expected on a vehicle with more than a million miles on the frame. This, along with a blown power steering unit, made every mile a battle. There was no relaxing, even on straight stretches. Occasionally the truck responded within normal expectations, a move he had decided now was simply to lull him into a false sense of security so that the '84 Chevy could quickly careen off the road, taking driver and load to a fiery death and perhaps some sort of mechanical peace for the suffering vehicle. Such observations kept him continually alert, but did make him consider if there was beginning to be a psychological toll as well as a physical one to this current endeavor.

"Anything I can do" he'd told his friend on one of his several trips to the VA hospital; "anything at all." Sincere in his offer to one whom had been a friend to his own family, as well as a soldier that had served his country and now a struggling small business

man---a *"jobber" that independently purchased fuel on the open market and distributed it to small independent gas stations, farmers, loggers and sawmills. Quite often these last three intermixed. In what were reported to be some of the poorest counties in this Midwestern state, numerous families had farms that they themselves logged the maturing timber and often turned the logs into various wood products right there on their own property---especially now that band saws were more efficient and affordable. These stops often called for deliveries of Off Road diesel for skidders, tractors, loaders and power plants, On Road diesel for pickups and log trucks, along with at least one gasoline product. Typically, none of the three to five hundred gallon farm tanks were marked to indicate which tank got which product. The wrong diesel could bring about a fine, diesel in a gas tank---a stopped vehicle, gas in a diesel tank a blown engine.*

"Anything" had become a phone call inquiring about his HAZMAT status. Still holding a Class A CDL that enabled him to drive eighteen-wheelers on down, and also currently with an endorsement to haul hazardous materials (why had he let only his bus passenger endorsement expire?), he was on the hook. Or ready to seize an opportunity to help, the perspective he held prior to bracing a wind chill factor now in single digits.

Curtis walked to the now encouraged fire, both warming himself and formulating his contribution to the latest topic. Like his two friends, his was a giving personality. He'd been raised poor, but in a community where poor just did not stand out. He was in high school when the majority of them had indoor plumbing; college when the first color television was watched there. They'd always joked while growing up that "if one of them had a dollar, they each had thirty-three cents."

"I built a back porch for my uncle. He'd been diagnosed with lung cancer, probably as much from smoking as from the years of welding stainless. Back then they were as ignorant of the toxicity of the fumes as a century earlier they'd been of mixing asbestos with plaster. Always a bachelor, he finally got on some program where a hospice worker came by every morning. Did a bit of cleaning and laundry. Even cooked a little. The cancer was taking its toll and soon Uncle Jim was either bedfast or in a recliner. More worrisome than his fulltime dependence on oxygen was his loss of hope. The shadow of death was as much a part of his small remote cabin as the grease stains in the kitchen or the gun racks and shoulder mounts in the living room. It was then while visiting one mid-afternoon that it came to me. He had been talking about when he'd first built the cabin, before he'd taken a welding job in the city. He wanted to build a back porch, off the kitchen and facing east in the morning. The view would have been much as the window above the sink, catching the early rays illuminating the tree covered ridge and then warming the small valley below. At first a shortage of funds and then later a shortage of time left the construction undone.

Well, I built the porch. Did the noisiest parts the days he was gone for radiation and chemo. Had it finished in less than a month. Complete with railings all around and a couple of Adirondack chairs. We started moving Jim out each day in time to watch the sunrise. Some days it took several blankets to keep him warm. But it gave him hope. He was not only looking forward to getting up each day, but was talking about the view of the foliage that coming fall; even the gobbling of turkeys the following spring. Seasons my uncle would not live to see, but seasons for which now he planned. Yes, that was without a doubt the best gift I ever gave."

The day had been a long one. Mid-morning had brought rain and a temperature slightly above freezing. Fog and condensation had battled with the slight downpour for control of the windshield, the result being the necessity to drive with one's head out the window. Conditions seemed insufferable until the afternoon's falling temperatures brought sleet and made the protrusion even more painful. Stops were now eagerly awaited, despite the increasing slipperiness of the truck's built-in ladder and the rungs attached to many of the tanks. At least there was no wind. That is until night fell. A northern wind drove the temperatures back into the teens and seemed to blow right through the insulated overalls and two coats. Gloves had to be removed in order to reset the counter on the pump, to fill out tickets and often to unlock padlocks from several of the farm tanks. At one of the last stops that night, he'd had to climb a tank at a sawmill that required a ladder. The requisite ladder was stored by the tank and both were now coated in ice. The mill was far from any other routes, so must be serviced. A hammer under the passenger seat was then used to strike at least some of the ice away, the summit achieved. Of course the cap was frozen solid, so another trip made down and back (only one fall, and this from one of the lowest rungs). The hammer was stuck in a back pocket, an adjustable wrench in the other. One hand of course held the nozzle and fuel line as he climbed, the other fought for a grip on the metal of the stand.

His hands were now in that abyss between every inch feeling penetrated by a dozen needles and there being no feeling at all. Operating the levers of the gates was becoming increasingly difficult though the gates themselves were relatively clear. There was no respite in the cab save protection from the wind, for the heater was as inoperable as the defrosters---both for the lack of a new heater core. Rubbing them together briskly increased both pain and dexterity. Finally the task was completed, the tank filled. To a lesser degree, the task was completed two more times---sans the need for the ladder. The first had been Off Road diesel, the next two On Road for their trucks and Premium for one of the owner's cars. This last seldom needed filling, but unfortunately had not been filled the last couple of weeks.

The trip home was arduous. The roads slick, visibility restricted, and breathing increasingly rough. Whether the cold air or the fumes, or the dangerous combination, each breath was both painful and not nearly enough. Sleet had turned to snow, a dangerous additive to an already existing layer of ice. Fear would have been a major part of his mindset had not the brain and body both already been numb. He fell as he exited the truck, fell again as he took the cardboard from his own vehicle's windshield. Finally getting the key into the door, and perhaps for the very first time truly appreciating the ingenuity of the remote start of later model vehicles, he watched the heat gauge with understandable anxiety. Whether it was the several ton difference in vehicle weight, the power being distributed to all four corners of the 4WD, or the fact that for the first time in hours he was no longer cold to the core--- driving his own vehicle felt almost like an out of body experience. He'd waited for the truck to warm, afraid his overtaxed and still shaking body not up yet to safely driving the three miles home. It would take soaking in a very warm tub of water and the drinking of two hot cups of tea before he could be described as warm. It would take nearly an hour before he fell asleep, mostly because he was running tomorrow's routes through his head. Trying to decide in advance how to load the multiple tanks for both trip efficiency and road safety, conscience of the load's effect on the truck's traction. A final thought was about the weather forecast he'd missed.

Steve smiled as he thought about the porch, and the boat.

"What about you?" Ben asked. "What was the best gift you ever gave?"

"How's it going so far?" the man asked, now at least able to sit up and partake of some of the VA's offerings other than Jell-O. His wife sat by his side, the hospital stay now on its second week. "The weather's been a little rough" offered the diminutive helpmate. "Hasn't it been quite cold?"

"Nothing too bad. I've got warm clothes."

"The truck doing okay? Running alright?" the former Army corporal inquired.

"Smooth as silk. Reminds me of my old logging days. It's all been kind of fun. My sincere thanks!" The trio laughed at the volunteer driver's show of gratitude.

"Yeah" Curtis chimed in. "What about it? What was the best gift you ever gave?"

Steve smiled. An involuntary shudder ran through his body as he recalled that month a few winters back. "Drove a truck for a guy once."

"Drove a truck? That was it?" challenged Ben.

"Yeah, I got to admit I expected a bit more. So you drove a truck for a guy, did you?" Again Curtis offered his two cents. "I must say, I'm a bit disappointed."

"Well, you should have seen the truck" Steve replied smiling. Yeah, he thought; even better, you should have tried driving it!

Check #1817

The card came from England, first correspondence they had ever recalled receiving from overseas. It was an expression of concern, included a quote about caring and then a few hand penned lines of love and encouragement. It came while the two were still in a motel, the fire loss only days old and an insurance settlement weeks away.

The sender was a college student, daughter of good, no, great friends. She was in every aspect their child. The work ethic, the pleasant countenance and constant willingness to share a smile. The sincere belief in a God that made all things possible; eventually all things good.

She was on a learning sojourn in Europe, part of an opportunity to study abroad and share her beliefs in Christ with those "from the old country." Several old countries. Born to parents stationed overseas, a father voluntarily continuing a heritage of military service; this was her first visit as an adult. A quite young adult.

Top grades and solid recommendations had made the event possible, along with her personal willingness to raise all of her projected expenses. As they read the card, the much older couple recalled the girl's solicitation concerning the trip this past summer. "Modest donations of money are accepted and greatly appreciated, but I ask for your prayers. For my safety, yes; but mostly that I have the grace, courage and wisdom to represent our Lord and our country as He would have me." A nice sentiment, especially as they knew it to be so sincere. The card coming from across the ocean did not surprise them. Her nightly call from her parents had informed her of the tragedy; her response appreciated but not surprising. Save for the enclosure.

The check was drawn on her hometown account. Number 1817 written for $400; a little Post It note explaining that this was all she could give as she still had to purchase her food for almost two months. She was on a possibly once in a lifetime adventure, and was giving away all of her discretionary funds and felt she needed to explain why she was not able to give more.

The man turned from his wife as he read the note, looked again at the amount on the check. A shirt sleeve dried the moisture which had formed at the corners of his eyes. He felt the hand on his shoulder; knew that she knew what he was thinking. Finally gave it voice. "She's really something! Of course, we cannot cash it."

The check, and the note, remain in an empty card box kept to house just such treasures. The couple did call the parents; procured the overseas number and called the girl. Expressed their heartfelt thanks. Later that night raised her up in their prayers and prayed for her future; secure in the assurance that "he who waters will be watered."

What's In A Name?

Utah looked at the imposing limestone bluffs. They had been reflecting the flames of campfires and the echoes of conversation for decades, as this was one of the more popular gathering spots on the Current River. William's Landing, it has served as a stopover for jonhboat float trips since the 1940's. Long owned by the Bunch family, the farm was known by locals as the Bunch Place. Utah was among many that wondered at the new name given the place by the park service.

Less than ten years previous the federal buying of land had begun; some purchases voluntarily from families tired of hard scrabble farming, others taken through the process of eminent domain. Family homes and community schools were destroyed, in some cases bulldozed and buried. Here, they merely changed the name.

Jerk Tail. Utah still laughed at hearing it. He'd "skinned" mules as a teenager, used "jerklines" and yelled "gee" and "haw" hundreds of times. Been trained by the son of a man whose father and uncle had actually helped build the base of what was now Highway 19 north of Eminence. Had never heard the phrase "jerk tail" until the National Park Service renamed this landing, explaining this was what freighters and farmers yelled to pulling teams headed up the steep roads exiting the valley.

To Utah, it would always be the Bunch Place. William's Landing. It was near the river that a man died. The infamous stabbing that forever unites those two families. A horrible resolution to a dispute over hogs. A dispute replicated several years later.

Lum Banks was tired of the hogs digging under his gate. Had even wrapped the lower board in barb wire to deter the half feral swine. He blamed Lloyd Randolph, for it was his notches in the offending sow's ear. So it was Lloyd Randolph Lum stabbed that fateful day.

This time death was averted. A young girl ran to the river, hailed a man with a johnboat. In less than two hours doctors had patched up Mr. Randolph and he would go on to lead a long life. As would Lum.

The Pay Check

It lay on the furthest corner of an upper bookcase, held in place by a spare clip from an old Model 788 Remington. The rifle itself was locked away in a gun vault, along with several boxes of 6mm cartridges, the round for which it was chambered. Dated six weeks back, Mark had long since decided not to deposit the more than three-hundred dollars. His account didn't necessarily need it, though his typical balance was not far above that figure. He'd made the money working for a gas jobber, a small LLC owned by a young couple struggling to make it in the fuel delivery business. As the third man in a three man operation, his job had been to fill up a single axle delivery truck with different fuels at the fledgling company's bulk plant.

The owner operated a similar vehicle, a tank truck with five separate compartments. Like Mark now, the owner filled up fuel tanks at small businesses, sawmills and farms. The number two guy drove the transport, picking up tanker loads of around 10,000 gallons of fuel and subsequently delivered to small independent gas stations and kept the company's bulk plant adequately stocked. Fuel was hauled and delivered as needed, and stockpiled to keep adequate supplies but also to attempt to take advantage of fluctuating markets. If fuel was on the rise, minimal supplies were purchased; storage tanks filled to the brim when product was less expensive.

Tim and Tina had started the business three years earlier, buying out a small jobber operating mainly in a single county. Almost two decades of working for a larger company had convinced the pair that financial security and job satisfaction lay down some other road. The first decade of their marriage had been in the service of their country, Tina following Tim to military posts on three separate continents. Thirty years and four children later they were working now to secure their retirement. Six work days and at least sixty hours were the norm.

Mark had got the call almost two months ago. A career with the state's Department of Education had come to an early end, retirement chosen after years of conflict with bureaucratic hierarchy. The entrenched waste and institutional inefficiency was more than he could take on a daily basis and, despite knowing all too well the career consequences, he was constantly at odds with his superiors. He had welcomed the call and quickly imagined becoming part of a growing business. The first week was spent learning loading and off-loading procedures while waiting for HAZMAT (Hazardous Material) and tanker endorsements to be added to his commercial driver's license. The second week he was behind the wheel and pleasantly surprised at how quickly the intricacies of driving a "working five" transmission came back to him. Occasionally there was a slight scraping of gears as the clutch-free upper range shifts were made.

Many of the customers he'd known from childhood. Sons of loggers now owned their own farms and sawmills, all requiring the delivery of varying fuels to their remote rural locations. A boat dock where he'd fished for decades at a nearby lake; a boat builder who heated their shop with their fuel oil. Ironically, the now very much retired gas jobber that had supplied the sawmill he himself had worked at as a teen-ager. A canoe vendor; a construction company adding a new lane to the local highway (here he fueled the equipment directly rather than a central storage tank). A transport company that purchased the green hued over the road diesel; a wood working shop that bought heating fuel for their buildings and Premium No-Lead for the family cars.

Even customers new to him, if not to the company, had many desirable traits in common. They were business people, the small businesses so often responsible for the majority of the growth in our country. "God-fearing folk", as an uncle used to say; the kind that depended upon their own hard work and ingenuity to survive and hopefully someday get a bit ahead. Much like the owners for whom he now worked. Such a contrast to the career-oriented, stab your co-worker in the back and forget all principles and morals crowd with whom he'd interacted with for decades.

The real trouble began the beginning of the third week. The headaches had been on and off for several days, merely a nuisance in his not-so-well informed opinion. It was the coughing that was getting to him. It had turned his throat raw and was depriving him of sleep, and much needed rest, at night. Thursday he saw a doctor; Friday he was seeing a specialist.

Though Mark had always considered himself fairly physically fit, despite years in a cubicle; he was not terribly surprised by what he now heard. A summer as a smokejumper had been both lucrative and exciting, but had left both a pair of vertebra and lungs in less than ideal condition. Notwithstanding a lifetime of healthy habits, his lungs had never fully recovered from a couple of close calls. The same incident that had damaged his lower back left him exposed to too much heat and toxic fumes from an abandoned pulp mill that had caught aflame.

The verdict was unanimous; the path ahead clear. The resignation brief and embarrassing; this had truly been his dream job. The small company paid bi-monthly, so one check was in the mail. It took a bit of persuasion to ensure there would be no other to cover the few more days worked.

Mark thought about framing the piece of financial commitment. He could hang it beside the hat on the wall. Or put it in the pocket of the company coat that, ordered over two months ago, had arrived just today.

Grandma's New Pet

Shelly took a final sip from the can of soda while parking the Chevy Tahoe in the shade. Two hours of driving now behind her, wishing for something perhaps a bit stronger than Diet Coke; she headed to the porch steps of the aging cabin. Nestled in a mature grove of short-leaf pine, the board and batten siding was gray save for the very tops given slight protection from the elements by the overhang of a shingled roof. One end of a clothesline was visible from just around the corner of the home, the wooden "T" leaning awkwardly towards the ground. Windows were opaque with dust and dried bugs, screens torn and rusted. A dwindling wood pile still took at least one-third of the porch.

The routine was always similar; Emily waited in their SUV while her mom checked out the porch scene. Though it had been four years since the "incident", she still could recall vividly the half-skinned bobcat hanging from beneath a rough sawn joist. The fact that her grandmother had "killed the varmint" to protect her small herd of Duroc swine did little to excuse what she considered the backward behavior of this hill dwelling relative. Selling the hide was more barbaric than capitalistic as far as the then twelve year-old was concerned. More than mere miles separated the extended family. A college degree and then a medical career had kept the daughter in the city her mother had only once visited. The granddaughter planned a similar career path, with perhaps a more advanced degree than her mother's Bachelors in Nursing. She had recently shadowed an anesthetist at her mother's place of work.

A nod from the mother let Emily know the coast was clear; no butchered mammals nor growling dogs. Grandmother Hayes sat quietly upon the porch, a small blanket of some sort in her lap. Shelly had closed the distance and was now taking the first of the three steps that would place her too on the plank floor. Emily had not accompanied her mother for more than a year, and knew to expect to find her grandmother's health even further deteriorated. Several members of the family had been discussing whether or not the eighty-seven year old could continue to live independently.

Shelly noticed something different. What she had taken for either a timeworn blanket or a furry coat was now squirming in her mother's lap. Her mother was trying to calm the animal as the third generation entered the scene.

"Why's grandma petting a possum?" inquired Emily with more calm than even she believed herself capable.

Sure enough, almost twenty pounds of adult marsupial was nestled in the lap of the elderly Hayes. She stroked his grayish fur; even ran her hand down the hairless, prehensile tail. Meanwhile, the curiosity of a sixteen-year old was not to be derailed.

"Grandma's petting a possum! Mom! I repeat, why's my grandma petting a possum?"

Shelly tried carefully to frame her response; herself both curious and concerned about the marsupial in her mother's lap. Not wishing to hurt her mother's feelings, nor to alarm and possibly agitate the wild animal; she whispered her response. Unfortunately it was drowned out by the words coming from the lady in the rocker.

Daughter and granddaughter simultaneously gasped as the Hayes matriarch continued.

"Fluffy's come back. After all these months, I'd given him up for dead. But just last night, I found him. I always set food out in his favorite dish, hoping against hope. And lo and behold, last night there he was. Eating just like old times. He's been eating good, fat as ever. But look, he's worn all the fur off his tail. Probably from chasing rats!"

This time Emily could hear her mother's whisper; her grandmother pausing for a breath, hands still stroking the grinning animal she cradled.

"Your grandma has cataracts, honey. I think they're getting worse."

This true and touching episode of Cataracts and Cats has been brought to you by Scales and Tails, *America's premier pet food. "If it ain't deep fried and then freeze dried; if cats don't purr and dogs demur----it ain't Scales and Tails." Keep watching for further episodes of everyone's most independent house pets overcoming the challenges of visual impediment. And yes, we continue to accept new sponsors. If interested, call BR 549 and ask for Sue Gato.*

A Half Century of Hunting Tails

The stove sat just to the right of the front room, a full wood box to its right and the black metal chimney rising from its center. To the left was The Beam. A hand hewn piece of cedar that had originally been the header for a barn door two miles up the creek. It had been salvaged and made part of the cabin when it was constructed in the late fifties, its ten foot span allowing the open floor plan into the kitchen. The red and white hues had darkened into yellows and browns and served as a muted backdrop for the more than hundred cloth ornaments nailed to the native wood.

"Are any of these yours?" I'd asked my host, Art. This was my first visit to a cabin older than I, its rustic setting on Little Blair's Creek now overshadowed by the decorations before me. I'd seen the pieces of garments in other cabins; sometimes on a mantle, often on a back wall. They often shared space with gun racks and mounted antlers, between framed photographs and outdated calendars.

"Sure are" he'd replied, and then pointed out a couple of square inches of faded red and black plaid. "I lost that in 1944. I was a big kid, happy that the war in Europe was going well and in a deer camp for the first time. I'd grown up on stories of just seeing a deer track, and my dad and I were just two of the over seven thousand that bought tags for the bucks-only newly reopened season. I remember hearing later less than six hundred were checked that year, so I didn't feel so bad about not filling my tag. But, sure enough, that second morning I missed a shot at one running through the brush. Wasn't even sure I saw horns, tried to get my Rocky Mountain peep sight on hair and fired. I levered another cartridge into my Winchester 30-30, but didn't get a second chance. My dad took that off my shirt tail when I got back to camp. Kept it in an old cigar box until I built this cabin a decade later. It was the first one up."

He walked across the pine boards, worn slick from years of being trod upon by boots and stocking foot alike, and stoked the fire. Placing two sticks of cherry wood on the now newly emboldened coals, he continued the tour.

"This white one was from my son. He was shooting a .25-06 about four hundred yards, missed a little eight-point basket rack. He'd made a similar shot on a spike buck the year before; should have known then the cancer was back. Last year he got to hunt. Still, I took that off a new cotton and denim western shirt he'd bought just for deer season." As Art momentarily turned away, I remembered his son's passing shortly after we'd met nearly ten years before.

Art started a pot of coffee, glanced back up at The Beam. Pointing to a bright orange patch, he again started. "This was Kyla's. My granddaughter. She was fourteen at the time and this was early nineties with doe tags available. We dressed her in orange almost head to toe, and this is from the Redhead shirt she was wearing. She and I were in my tree stand overlooking a grove of white oak up on the flat. She shot at two does with a Remington .243 we'd given her as an early Christmas gift. The 742 semi-automatic had little kick and she'd been practicing for over a month. She killed one, but had missed the first one she shot at; insisted we cut off her shirt tail and add it to the collection as tradition demanded." I'd met this lady, now a mother herself; and could easily imagine her insistence at being treated as "one of the boys."

He showed me the brown corduroy that was worn by Adam, fresh back from Iraq two years ago and glad to have missed in a less tumultuous and deadly situation; the olive Filson wool hunting shirt that the local banker had to be held while the patch of shirttail was removed, he complaining it was a several hundred dollar garment. The more recent included trophies from archery and muzzle loading seasons, as well as firearms. Many were from friends, most were from family.

"I've got a hammer and an eight penny nail ready, just in case" Art reminded me. Though confident in my Sako *Forrester*, I still had a moment of regret that I'd worn a new shirt that morning.

Cutting a hunter's shirt tail off when they miss has long been an Ozark tradition. Art has now passed, but shirttails continue to be placed on the wall of the cabin. Numerous hunting cabins have long had their exteriors adorned with the antlers of our prey, but many times some of the best tales are told with cloth.

American Heroes---"The Jack Roberts Episode"

It was cold. Men were without shoes for the snow covered forests. The flame of liberty flickered as the British troops, reinforced by Hessian mercenaries, were sitting proud in the city of Trenton. But one man had a plan. One man defied the odds and drove his troops to the point of physical exhaustion. On a cold Christmas night he crossed the Delaware River, out flanked the Redcoats and black hearted killers for hire; soundly defeating them and giving both victory and hope to the American Army of the Revolution. The date was December 25, 1776. The man was George Washington.

A century later man was still dependent for his news on the printed word. Just as it had taken nearly four months for the election of our third president to reach west of the Mississippi, it took weeks for farmers to know market prices within the same state. Families went to bed mad because of all the hollering. Children lived in constant fear of their parents divorcing simply because dad had stayed too late at the tavern or mom too long at a quiltin' and the abandoned spouse hollered until their lungs almost burst trying to toll them home. Then one man jumped communication a giant yodel forward as assistant Watson was called via wires into an adjoining room. The date was March 10, 1876. The man was Alexander Graham Bell.

Millions of families were trying to recover from the after effects of Wall Street speculators. Many were still without jobs. Men left their homes in search of employment; sometimes for a day, at other times for weeks or months. Women were struggling to take up the slack; inevitably things suffered. Children weren't read to from the Holy Book as often, watered down gravy was poured over stale bread from the meal the evening before. Then, once again, someone defied the odds. Boldly stepped forward and met the challenge with courage and innovation. Flour dough was pre-mixed and stuffed into foil wrapped wax paper and slid ten pre-cut circles at a time into tubes of cardboard. Though the purchase of Ballard Flour Company by Pillsbury later would make these modern conveniences standard fare among all the land, people in Louisville, Kentucky were able to rap these paper cylinders against a hard edge, place the white orbs on a greased pan and in minutes have golden topped biscuits from a can. The date was 1931. The man was master baker Lively B. Willoughby.

Thousands of Americans were in their backyards each evening; focusing telescopes and adjusting binoculars in preparation of dark. Anxiously, more so in trepidation than eagerness, awaiting a glimpse of the reflections from a small device now orbiting our atmosphere. The suns' rays off the metal skin of the Russian satellite had created great distress among first the Washington politicians, then the Pentagon generals and even scientists of the entire Western Hemisphere. Now all of the United States was caught up in Sputnik distress, wondering if indeed the Communists had solely conquered the skies, and if they had, would this perhaps lead to the Red Menace domination of the world?

Then, from among a host of daring young men who had made challenging the dangers of the sky their lives' work, another atmospheric gladiator stepped forward. Boarding a missile which had numerous predecessors exploding on the launch pad, he climbed into a capsule little larger than a fat man's coffin and ended up orbiting our earth in Friendship 7. The United States was again on top in the Space Race and children could study their math books in peace. The date was February 20, 1962. The man was John Glen.

We turn now to a more modern time. Once again speculators have driven up the price of commodities-----gasoline appears to be headed toward an unheard of $5 per gallon. WWII vets like Bob Massey wonder how much more strain the household budget can stand. A man whom left home at an early age to fight for his country and the cause of liberty on this planet. A man whom spent months standing guard in a land devastated by globalistic greed; he part of the bastion of hope for a defeated people trying to restart their lives and rebuild their nation. Scantly a mile down the road retired teacher Judy Mansfield wonders how much of the family budget will be spent by her wandering husband ever in search of a story to tell. Wondering if he will get them from scribbled notes to a marketable format, and if so, will someone buy them.

Both have one thing in common. Well, I guess, two. First, how soon can they get their gardens in this wildly warm spring? But second, they both yearn for a batch of fresh fish. Some succulent white fleshed crappie encrusted in golden brown meal, fresh from a pot of heated grease; served perhaps with a few fried potatoes and onions. Accompanied by cornbread hot from a cast iron skillet; made with the same fresh ground meal that covered the aquatic cuisine. But it seemed these two worthy Missourians were destined to make due with mud ditch raised catfish served on Friday buffets. March winds were stronger than normal and even diminutive ponds in the most serene of settings were being thrashed into white caps. Lakes large enough to play host to significant crappie populations had waves that were making Gordon Lightfoot consider cutting a new album. Fresh crappie, at least for the present, were out of the question. A hopeful pedagogue and trusting warrior were to be denied, or so it seemed. Again, as so often when this great nation appeared headed to her knees; there appeared a hero. A man whose abilities far surpassed the challenges of Mother Nature. True, normal men, even kids, can catch spring crappie on a pretty day. But when howling wind and treacherous wave kept the fainthearted in port, blackened skies and swirling current caused lines to tangle and hearts to quiver; one man separated himself from the crowd. Placing fealty and honor before any consideration of fear; service to others above personal health and well-being, he took to the sea (or at least a really nice private lake). Defying common logic, going against even

"In-Fisherman" episodes and Wally Marshall seminars; he sailed (well---a 60/40 Mercury Jet atop a 20/56 Blazer boat from Ernie's Sales and Service helped) forth with baited breath---and hook. That evening Judy and Bob, and their families, ate their fill of delicious, sun brown delicacies with all the trimmings. The date was March 6, 2012. The man, Jack Roberts.

This week's episode of American Heroes was brought to you by Ellington's own Blazer Boats. "If you ain't fishin' Blazer, you ain't fishin' the best!" Join us again next week when American Heroes presents important, but often lesser known, warriors for liberty. That sponsor to be announced at a later date. Anyone interested call Junior at BR-549. Thanks and have a great day!

A Riverman's Legacy

He sat in the old paisley upholstered chair, his bending posture only a slight detraction of the man whom had so long stood a full head above the majority of his peers. A stroke had left a leg refusing its submission to his will; though his mind was as clear as his blue eyes and the hands that held the cooling cup of coffee revealed the physical strength that had poled jon boats up and down Current River, had split firewood and for several decades pulled a ferry. Still, he found himself away from his home and residing in this single-bed room of a small town nursing facility. Decorations were sparse, the King James Bible the most prominent item on his nightstand. A long-time member of a local Baptist Church, it was not only fodder for nightly reading but symbolically stood for the creed of no alcohol nor tobacco he'd adhered to since marrying his childhood sweetheart. It was in this room that Bill visited him each week.

They'd first met when he'd come to the Ozarks as a young ranger. It seemed Buck epitomized the culture and life Bill had come to protect, the aging local having been raised on the very river Federal statutes now sought to regulate. His business was now in the hands of a son and grandson. The small store and canoe livery was blossoming under the increased activity growing from the national recognition of the spring fed stream. He sat resigned to his fate; but continued the same request as before.

"Hey, Bill; did you bring me that drink of water?" Buck had made the same request each of Bill's weekly visits, just as he made the request from his own son when he visited. The elder Maggard had grown up sipping constantly from the clear water of the Current River. When they built the ferry that carried people, cars and trucks from one side of the river to the other, he'd driven a galvanized nail into the upstream railing. Upon that nail hung a tin ladle, one that had been in his family for as long as he could remember. He'd used it on a regular basis to quench his thirst when either operating the wood structure or just in its near vicinity.

Bill always made some excuse for having forgot it; privately bowing to the wishes of Buck's family and physicians that were adamant about the patriarch only drinking distilled or chlorinated water, and certainly not from the bug ridden aquifer that played host to fish and fowl. During these visits, once past the awkwardness of the initial request; they would reminisce about their early encounters. Bill would trade stories of current happenings for tales of Shannon County's waterways in the past.

Just as rivers flow towards the sea and sycamores grow from saplings to stately guardians of their banks and then someday must fall; old age presents a bill that must be paid. At last, one summer; a visit from Buck's son was to take place in a nearby hospital in an adjoining town. Perhaps feeling himself the end was near; or maybe looking ever forward and fortified by his lifelong belief in the healing qualities of the water he'd so often lifted via tin cup to his thirsting lips; he again made the request. And again was denied.

Here, the story veers to a different path. A young doctor, new to the patient but not to the impending outcome of the unraveling events; assured Buck's son of its medical neutrality.

"If I could grant my dying father such an easy boon, I'd get him the water!" he'd assured him.

Buck's son sprang to action. Getting his own son on the phone back at their business; orders were quickly delivered and acted upon. Grandson Marcus went to the basement, found a clean quart Mason canning jar complete with lid, and went down to the ferry. He even used the old metal ladle and filled the jug nearly to the top. The lid secured, he wrapped the vessel in a shirt, jumped into a company truck and headed north to the hospital. Making the near hour long drive as rapidly as safely possible; he parked, ran to an elevator and moments later burst into his grandfather's room to present the cool liquid.

Silence echoed from the ivory walls; Eugene greeting his son with a stoicism refined during the past half-minute since Buck had been pronounced. An inner strength of his own kept the young man from dropping the treasured delivery; realization his gift could not now be delivered raced through him as a knife into his heart. But Ozark resilience is a strong commodity and hillbilly ingenuity a resource not to be denied. Buck's progeny were not yet done.

Two days later, Bill stood in line at the memorial. Though a few visitors were ahead of him in line beside the coffin; he could clearly see the Mason jar and its crystalline contents nestled in the old riverman's right arm. Knowing quite well the history behind this loving gesture, his solemn reflection was interrupted by the pair of elderly ladies immediately before him. As they both peered into the oak structure that contained the mortal remains of their friend, one could be heard crisply stating to the other, "I never knew Buck Maggard was a moonshiner!" The response was immediate. "All those old Shannon County men were moonshiners."

The Stand

C.W. came by early, even by his own accounts. True, he'd warned a day or so back he'd be stopping by and "engagin' my help fer a spell." Nearly three decades of friendship had taught me C.W. was an early riser. When he'd stop by to give me a ride to the deer woods, a five AM assignation was more like 4, or even 3:30. Contrary to the wisdom that "old people required less sleep", he'd been gathering eggs and frying them hours before the rooster heralded the break of day for most of his life. Anyway, I awoke at 5 AM and was finished tying my bootlaces as C.W.'s bent but not broken four-wheel drive pulled into my driveway.

A brief conversation revealed he sought help putting up a tree stand for the upcoming deer season.

"When we were working in yer shop last summer, didn't I see an extra deer stand hangin' 'round?" We'd worked earlier on a wooden jonboat we hoped to complete this decade.

After informing him I even had a brand-new ladder stand still in the box, I stuck some tools in my overall's pockets, loaded the unopened parcel and we headed to Blair's Creek. A novice might have trouble finding the white oak haven on Wildcat Flats where the "new-fangled, store bought outfit" was to be placed, but muscle memory took over and in moments we were at the base of a tall, straight black oak just downwind of the stand of its fairer barked cousins. As our luck would have it, the combination of CW and I attempting something in the outdoors seemed somehow to always tempt the fates, a predicted fall rain coming thirty-six hours early.

"Don't worry CW, we'll just leave the whole box here at the base of the tree and put 'er up pre-dawn Saturday."

"Think it'll be that easy?" CW was well aware of our past history.

"I've put these up before. There's like eight pages of pictures and really good instructions. The proverbial piece of cake!" Even I was assured of our imminent success.

Fast-forward to a week later, little cap bill lights in place, we brushed the leaves away from the previously hidden package of cardboard. At least two hours separated us from daybreak; plenty of time to assemble the stand and let the air born molecules of sweat dissipate into the early morning. Fate not being a mistress to leave unattended, it was then we noticed the small hole in the corner of the box. A few strokes of a recently sharpened skinning knife and the pieces were loosened, the bag of nuts and bolts revealed, and a large nest of what were mere days ago explicit directions now hosted the small droppings familiar in most mouse nests.

Two great minds were now challenged, and rose to meet that challenge just as Achilles rose to do battle in the Trojan War; just as heroically and just as doomed. Whether or not the destruction of both sets of lights as two heads smashed together was the final straw will never be known, but time demanded immediate results so I was on my crossing as the first lights of dawn broke over the eastern ridge. CW admitted the stand turned out to be more comfortable than he'd expected from "something designed in a cubicle and built in China" and swore his gratitude for its loan despite the many rounds of laughter later at his expense. Seems that as he was finally assured the stand was successfully assembled and attached to the tree, he placed his seventy-six year old frame upon the "comfortable hunter-friendly" repose. As full sun illuminated the Ozark landscape, friends heading later to their crossings noted a man seated barely two-feet off leaf covered soil, his stance braced against the ground by what was supposed to have been a shooting rest and adorned by a dozen metal steps reaching far above into the favored oak.

The Check

It lay on the desk, amidst ironically an unpaid bill for my subscription to *Field & Stream* and a half-written letter to a friend. More of a note really; part of an effort to mail a letter a day as they struggled with the absence from their hometown midst their freshman year of college. One of several young people we attempt to encourage long-distance, she was perhaps a bit special. Maybe even quite special; but back to the check.

Amber in color and longer in length than my personal ones, it was a business check from the local funeral home. The amount was modest by some standards, though a brief trip down memory lane recalled many a time it would have been most significant. One hundred dollars. Hardly the month's interest on what was left of my mortgage, but a tidy sum for what some might say was less than an hour's work.

I'd received the call mid-morning. The minister scheduled for the next day's funeral had taken ill, I was asked to fill in. The opportunity actually consisted of several hours of preparation. Visiting with family and friends at that evening's visitation. Confirming facts for the reading of the obituary. Collecting anecdotes that would better personalize the service; capture the man being honored and best do his life honor. Later that night I would spend several hours roughing out and refining a draft, selecting Scripture I believed most appropriate. Construct phrases that hopefully would bring both closure and solace to the family. True enough, the service itself was much less than an hour. So, in some ways, a hundred bucks an hour. Not bad work if you can get it.

Trouble with the check was not in the amount---more than fair; nor the payer---he was comfortable enough to easily afford it. Nor in its source, as the owner explained—a good Christian man by the way----this was a prepaid funeral and the money had actually been in an account for decades. No, the problem was the "services delivered." I "came to the party late" you might say, as to my more formalized relationship with God. Baptized in my early thirties, one of my first opportunities of service was to preach the funeral of a dear friend. A young mother with whom I'd shared a childhood; shared even that transition we all make awkwardly into adulthood. Cancer had stolen all of her tomorrows. I asked God for the strength to get through the service, for the wisdom to find and deliver the proper words. I vowed to myself, perhaps even Him---my memory is vague, to never profit from such service.

This last might seem a bit strange, but keep in mind I came from, if not unbelievers, certainly non-practitioners. My experience with preachers was that as a general rule they were fat, loud and blatant hypocrites. At a tender age I'd suspected that the majority were not ardent fans of manual labor and that there was a distinct correlation between hot summers and young men being "called" to the pulpit. Later I noticed a similar relationship concerning layoffs at the local mines and the sudden conversions to the ministry.

Already known for working multiple jobs the majority of my life; I did not wish that friends be tempted to place my recent efforts in a similar capitalistic category.

Hence my problem with the check. So on my desk it remained, now the nucleus of several sheets of unfinished business. After a few days the magazine invoice was joined by an invitation to an environmental workshop and a reminder of a Housing Authority board meeting coming later in the month, an obligation I'd only recently accepted. The first note was finished and gone; several successors took its place. In time they also were finished and mailed, the meeting attended, the subscription renewed.

By the second week, the check had made it from the pile to a more organized stack. During that time we had taken my widowed mother for a trip to the city, including dinner at a fine steakhouse and theatre tickets. She was well entertained, I'd continued to fulfill a deathbed promise to my dad, and the coffers were a wee bit leaner. Then there was the trip to the vet.

It's not every day that a beagle spends three days in a hospital, but this dog was much more than a great hunter. He was as much family, as far as our hearts were concerned, as those sharing my name and blood. Several liters of IV drips and some bladder therapy (still not sure what that was) later and he was better. Not good as new, mind you. But better. Things were looking up. Balances were going down. The check was curling at the edges.

The call from my brother was unexpected. Predictable; just unexpected. Four years ago I'd heard from him when he needed a new well pump. Two years ago his car was in the shop. Two days ago his electric was about to be shut-off. As in the previous occurrences, he was ready with account numbers, specific debts and deadlines. His faith was to be admired; my gullibility questioned. His lights stayed on; my con detector went off. An intrusive breeze took advantage of an opened door, the check blown to the floor.

Yesterday I worked in my office. Paid my mother's rent—that Housing thing for Seniors to which I now have the honor of helping to direct. Mainly I was there to meet my own deadlines. Writing deadlines at local papers. I'm a columnist. Maybe with this material my readership would be increasing. Certainly my resources were decreasing. I considered all this as I picked the dust-covered pledge of future payment from the tiled floor. A push pin placed it alongside the picture of my niece and her three-and-a-half pound trout. That latest trip's cost would be coming in the mail soon, courtesy of the *VISA* accounting department. These two items stood in stark contrast to the yellowing index cards that dominated the corkboard, they the skeletal beginnings of a novel now several years in the making.

I began the day having to borrow the electrical energies of my wife's fairly new GMC pickup to jumpstart my own vehicle built two decades past. Seems though the *Ever Ready Bunny* keeps on going and going, Sears Die Hards have their limits. Small towns have their limits as well as their wonderments, their bargains and their less-than-bargains. An hour later I was writing a hundred and three dollar check for what was possibly some of China's best work. Returning home, I went to my office and balanced my account. Before me were numbers documenting what I was fairly sure of; I was stressing my reserves. Just above the black and white confirmation of my fiscal demise was the check. And the smiling niece. And the crimson-sided rainbow trout reminding me of the next promised trip only weeks away.

Now principles are a great thing. More easily adhered to when larders overflow than when one is having to "water down the soup." I had vowed to never profit from direct service to my Lord. Not for preaching Sundays when a church was in need, not for "marrying people off" to begin life anew. Not for "speaking words over them" as a life has come to an end. Not even when hand digging the actual place of internment. Principle. Possibly overdrawn account. Reality.

To be honest, or at the least to try; I could not remember exactly to whom I'd made the vow. If it were to me alone; well, unfortunately, I'd lied to myself before. As I pulled the pin from the cork, and placed the now un-impaled item in my pocket; I vaguely recalled cashing a check for a wedding some several years back, at the much inebriated father of the bride's insistence. Precedence.

Alternate ending:

    To be fair, although I couldn't remember to whom I'd made the vow, it was nevertheless a commitment. The metal no longer holding the item to the wall, I placed it in my pocket. Perhaps it would bolster my resolve as later that day I returned the check. Remind me of both the blessing and responsibility we are given by the presence of the young. Promise.

Healing Waters

Laura was still becoming accustomed to her set of duties in this remote outpost. She viewed this place much as some of the military settings of Rudyard Kipling, her latest favorite author. She'd first been exposed to his prose in *Stalky & Co.* and though it was set at a boys' boarding school, had found common ground with her experiences at Central Hospital where she spent three years in the St. Louis nursing school. *Captains Courageous* had in part inspired her to set out on her own, leaving the security of friends and family to be a working girl. She'd taken the job in this isolated rural hospital after attending a weekend seminar on asthma and possible treatments. She'd met Dr. Diehl and been inspired to become part of something new.

The bus ride from St. Louis had been long and fairly uneventful. The final stop was at Salem. She'd offloaded with a few other passengers. A woman and her daughter whom had been at a clinic for blindness. A businessman seeking more urban consumers for his barrels, the expanding distilleries a promising market. A farmer and his wife seeing a son off at Union Station.

She wore one set of clothes; two more were in the leather satchel that had ridden the more than hundred miles under her seat. A comb and brush set from her high school graduation, a copy of the New Testament given by the Gideons the same occassion. *The Jungle Book* and *Just So Stories* had accompanied her as well.

Laura had actually reached her final destination by team and wagon. A local farmer bringing home flour and canning supplies had been found going in the same general direction. The last mile she walked.

Welch Spring Hospital was a combination resort and sanitarium. The Illinois doctor believed in the healing power of the cool air coming from the mouth of the cave from which poured forth the spring. He had built the hospital to actually capture the air and circulate it throughout the patient's rooms. There was also a lodge and a couple of cabins. Though not the main emphasis, tourism was accommodated. In fact, catered to.

Current River had been a destination of fisherman for some time. Round Spring State Park was over a decade old and Highway 19 had been constructed all the way to Eminence. Organizations such as the Shannon County Hunting and Fishing Club encouraged trips to the pristine area, despite the primitive level of available roads.

Laura Dunn was twenty-seven, just turned. The Ozark spring was just coming alive, with redbuds emerging from dormancy and dogwood shrubs just getting the first tints of green on the branch's twigs. Her chores ranged from updating the charts of patients, as hospital occupancy demanded; to cleaning cabins and changing linen in guest's rooms as well. She did laundry and even shared cooking and dishwashing duties when the patient load was down.

This was planting time, as with most of the adjoining native homesteads they tried to be as self-sufficient as possible. Potatoes were already in the ground, had been for over a week. With a last name like Dunn, it seemed growing the Irish staple was in her blood. She hoped this year to add sweet corn in addition to the Hickory Cane they grew for livestock and meal. Just the past season she'd added Brandywine tomatoes to the bi-color German variety that had been handed down in her family for generations.

She remained in awe of the ingenuity displayed by locals. The most recent innovation was a cable strung across the river just below where the spring entered. The farmer from across the way had rigged a pulley system and now and again drew a burlap wrapped packet out and lowered it into the rapids at the head of the shoal, often leaving it submerged for hours. Curiosity had got the best of her and she'd asked. Inside several layers of burlap sacks was a gallon jar with buttermilk. The tumultuous river did the churning and they would later retrieve butter.

The day was full of promise as she noticed a new chart. A Mr. Frank Brown. She immediately felt a bit of distant kinship. From her studies, as well as personal history, she knew that Brown was the Anglicized form of Braun, an old German name. Her own name, Dunn, was Irish for the very same color. Yes, 1936 was going to be a great year!

Frank Brown's route to the collection of stone and timber structures adjacent to the spring fed stream had been a bit more complex, both in time and geography. Much like Ms. Dunn, he'd been born in the same state. Just further south. She had been born in a new brick home on Cherry Street in Maplewood in 1909. The family was proud of its economic ascendance, Laura's father having been born in Dogtown and risen from a small family coal mining operation to foreman of a brick factory in a few short decades.

Frank had been born in the same era as Laura's father. Only his family owned neither a home nor a business, no matter how small. Frank's father had come over during the German Revolution of 1848, married a fellow immigrant and fought for the Union in our own Civil War. He'd worked construction after the war and his two sons followed suit.

Frank's first job away from family was the rehabilitation of the *Des Peres* stream and the clearing of land for the Louisiana Purchase Exposition. He helped construct the Palace of Agriculture, a temporary structure that covered twenty-three acres of ground. He worked on the Pike, a mile of varying amusements during the 1904 event. When work finally ended with the dismantling of the majority of the buildings, he sought new sights. New seas. At first he worked river boats and landed a job on a tug going from New Orleans to Dubuque. Then freighters to South America and eventually Europe.

These experiences enticed the US Navy into offering him enlistment as Firemen First Class in the early summer of 1917. He found himself again working with the coal of his tugboat days, as the ship on which he served had as yet to be converted to more efficient oil burning furnaces. His first assignment, the US Lenape, was a cruise ship hastily converted to troop transport. Later he would serve on the US Fanning, a destroyer escorting such ships. He was aboard when she sank the German submarine U-58, a moment of self-awareness and reflection when one of the surrendering enemy was brought aboard and the name Braun could be easily read on his uniform.

After the Great War, he was mustered out and worked on commercial freighters once again. Always in the bowels of the steel leviathans, working his way up to the job of diesel mechanic as ships were continually updated to the hotter burning fuel.

He was in port in Galveston when he first collapsed. The Great Depression almost behind them, the oil business in Texas offered opportunity to regain his land legs and breathe more open air. Still, the shortness of breath remained as did the chest pain. The constant tiredness. A trip to his birthplace brought him the best that Midwest medicine could offer. It was when he could not pass a physical to get back on a river boat that he knew he needed more. It was then he heard of the work of Dr. Diehl.

"Good morning!" Laura found Mr. Brown in his room. He had a copy of Whitman's *Leaves of Grass* in his lap. He hurriedly stood as she entered the room.

"The door was open. I hope I'm not intruding." She noticed the military bearing, had briefly reviewed his chart. Noted that the war experience was just one of many jobs that had been a threat to his lungs. The construction including the application of plaster, the time spent shoveling coal. The diesel fumes as a mechanic. He'd compounded it all with heavy smoking. Never married, no immediate family. She smiled, waiting an answer. Noticed the copy of Thoreau's *Walden: Life in the Woods* lying neatly on the small oak desk. The pen and paper arranged uniformly along with a watch and billfold. A glance into an open closet revealed clothes all on hangers, socks and underclothes folded and stored on the upper shelf. His voice was a pleasant interruption to what she was afraid was becoming an unintended invasion of his privacy.

"Not at all. Please come in. I'm Frank Brown. Please call me Frank." He found he was saying more than he'd intended, in part to perhaps put her at ease, he sensed a bit of discomfort. He also spoke as he sized her up. She was tall, nothing like his six five; but probably at least five ten. Her hair was the auburn of African sands aglow beneath a setting sun; her eyes the green of the hills of Ireland herself. They reminded him of dew strewn fern catching a ray of summer sunshine.

The two talked nearly an hour. She explained the protocol, the times for meals and the encouragement to spend the warmer part of the days in the room with the fresh air circulating. Treatment consisted mainly of rest. Medications were largely a simpler diet and lots of herbal teas.

They had found they had much in common. Laura left and resumed her other chores, including charting a couple of other patients.

Summer in the Ozarks was beautiful that year. Laura's garden was doing great, the sweet corn was preparing to tassel, potatoes had bloomed well and pole beans were beginning to bear. Already she had gathered enough gooseberries for a pie. Blackberries would follow soon.

They sat quietly on one of the wooden tables overlooking the river. They'd just come from the dining room in the lodge. The guests and patients had eaten together, there being few of either group. After the evening meal most returned to their individual rooms.

Laura and Frank had fallen into a pattern; a daily routine. After the evening meal they took a walk along the river, frequently climbing some of the paths that provided a view of the valley and the fields just across the river. This was haying season, and the smell of freshly mown grass mingled with the aromas native to the local flora. Sounds included the melodic tinkling of the spring breaking over the dam and entering the main body of the river. The bird calls, including whippoorwills, were becoming more prevalent as the evenings warmed.

"The pie was delicious" Frank commented, in a voice Laura now realized was softened as much by personality as by physical deterioration. Over the past couple of months she'd seen some change, an increased endurance on their walks, a more noticeable lightness in his step. The voice remained gentle. Sure and firm in tone and content; if anything there was an essence of even deeper humility. There had always been a certain unpretentiousness about him; now it seemed he spent more time in self-reflection.

"I'm glad you liked it. I've noticed you no longer carry Whitman, that Thoreau now accompanies us on these walks." Laura knew that he read often in his room, and that he usually had one of his two books in a jacket pocket.

"Not that I have gleaned all, or even most, of the wisdom these word impart; but I have studied them closely. Took note of context; searched for nuance. I fear my lungs may have been the least of my concerns if I would have examined my life more closely. I saw the wonders of the world while somehow missing the beauty of Creation." Again, Frank found himself speaking more than he'd intended. He looked away as he became silent.

"Did you find more answers in the poetry or the prose?" Laura was familiar with both authors, had read a bit of both works.

"I found more questions than answers in them both. Not sure which to reread next." He looked back upon her countenance as he spoke. Were there perhaps keys to life's mysteries in the emerald orbs before him?

Laura returned his gaze. Frank seemed even more pensive than he'd been of late. She wondered if she should make the offer, not wanting to threaten the friendship that was clearly developing. Age and experience had shaped their relationship as more of a niece to an uncle, but it held forth the promise of a closeness that she was growing to treasure. Still, something encouraged her.

"I have something you might enjoy. A gift my Senior year in high school."

The moon was a pale silver, washing the countryside with a serene chromatic hue. It was August and the nights still warm. They'd walked to the hole above the outlet of the spring, on a small gravel bar where they'd spent several afternoons swimming the past few weeks.

They'd waded out waist deep, allowed themselves a moment to acclimate to the coolness of the stream. Laura stepped closer, placing one hand beneath Frank's lower back and permitting him to grasp her other in the two of his.

"Do you accept Jesus Christ as your Lord and Savior, and now wish to be symbolically buried and resurrected in obedience to His Gospel?" She trembled slightly as she asked, and not from any cold. She recalled her own similar experience when seventeen, a decade ago. Hers had been in a warmed baptistery and by an elder member of the church. She had never been party to such activities in the wild, as it were; though since coming here she had heard of them.

"Yes. Yes, I do so wish." Frank closed his eyes as she lowered him into the water, was unaware of the cold as he was completely submersed and then brought back upright. A younger man might well have been more aware of the physical charms of the woman who held him, the maturing bosom so near his cheek, the fine bones of the hand that had held his, the lithe limbs that had raised him forth. All Frank felt was a strange sense of belonging, as if the world he'd been trying to understand was welcoming him as a part.

After a brief prayer they walked back to their respective rooms. The next morning neither spoke of the prior evening's occurrence. Within a week Frank was leaving. Their parting was brief, Frank taking advantage of his height to bestow a fatherly kiss upon her forehead. Laura watched him shoulder his pack and leave; noticed his glance backward as he crested the nearest ridge. In his billfold was her address; he was unable to do likewise because of the uncertainty of his plans.

Laura finished the summer by preparing for the harvest. Corn was canned along with beans, some stored dried on the cob to be shelled and ground later for meal. A few more patients came and went, as did several fall fishermen. She missed Frank, remembered well his parting words.

"You helped to give me a new life. A better life. How I can ever thank you, I do not know. I will raise you up in prayer each and every day. As you awake each dawn, know that you are the subject of my prayers."

Laura thought of that daily, wondered from where her name had been elevated in spiritual petition. Often it caused a brief moment of sadness; always renewed encouragement. Over time it became a part of every day, the wonder of his possible location. The chance they might see each other again.

Laura would marry the following summer. A young man from a nearby farm. She would work there for four more years, until the death of Dr. Diehl brought about the closing of the facility and the selling of the property. During that time she'd received several cards from Frank; brief summaries of a continued life of adventure.

Frank remained tied to the sea, now working topside in whatever capacities he could attain. Nearly three months before the

Japanese attack on Pearl Harbor, he was one of the twenty-six crewmen lost when the freighter *Montana* was torpedoed and sunk in

the North Atlantic. Injured by the initial explosions, he drowned pulling another sailor to safety. His Gideon copy of the New Testament in his pocket; Laura's address in his billfold. Only hours before he'd begun the day in prayer, lifting up her name as was his daily custom.

Fifty Dollars

The legs would go first, that he remembered. He was in the third round of a ten round prelim. His jabs still had plenty of snap, his breathing not yet labored. He'd gone to the body the last couple of minutes, his internal clock telling him that in about twenty seconds the bell would ring. Enough time for another series of punches. A quick combination of feinting jabs to the head and then hooking back to the body. He brought two hard rights into his opponent's diaphragm, turning him perfectly for the strong left to the kidneys. The bell rang as he was setting his feet for another series.

He strode to the corner thinking he'd been ready for the headshots. Now the same minute of rest he was receiving would be allowing the man in the opposite corner to recoup; the same wet sponge wiping the sweat from their shoulders, the same bottle of water sweeping the spit and blood from their mouths. He'd need to start over, to literally pummel the heart from this fighter, to set him up for the knockout. He'd need the knockout. He'd need it soon, because of the legs.

The run was only three miles. He got it in almost every evening, usually right after work and before cleaning up for an evening out with his friends. A half-mile of almost level ground, up a small incline, a quarter-mile of gentle swag where the gravel road crossed the head of a hollow, and then the Hill. Nearly sixty degrees of incline, it was as fearsome in the descent as it was formidable in the climb. He was always careful to run in the most heavily traveled pathways, leery of loose pebbles and rocks that could lead to his demise. There was about two hundred feet of level ground before the wet weather creek dissected the road. Two hundred feet he usually ran backwards to work on his calves. Two hundred feet of relative physical calm prior to starting the climb. Then back up, this time without the fear of falling but burning in his lungs as air came in sharp rasps. The pain in knees that had been too often stressed by the shouldering of extreme weights; even further abused by summers of rodeo fun and eight-second bouts matched against Brahma bulls and bucking broncs.

Once the Hill was ascended, the dip and then flat ground. If he was feeling especially confident, or combative, he ran the majority of this backwards as well. The nature of his work, along with a steady regimen of push-ups each morning as he rolled out of bed, pretty much assured him of the ability to throw punches. Hard punches. It was the legs he worried about.

He tucked his elbows tight against his own body, gloves covering his face as he fought for breath. His opponent was tired, he could tell from the flailing from which he was defending himself. The blows were slung more than thrown; desperate more than deliberate. Though it might very well appear to the untrained eye as dancing around, the footwork of his adversary lacked both artistry and purpose. To a degree it helped maintain the appearance of a moving target, but it was not providing a stable platform from which to launch a meaningful assault. In fact, he was pretty sure that he'd figured out what little pattern there was to the sporadic movement. The opponent would circle to the fighter's right, perhaps weary of the left hook that had been landing successfully to the body. And then he'd close; becoming as much a target as a weapon.

The fifth round was almost over. He wanted the knockout, but was careful to maintain whatever point lead he might have accumulated. As the blows to his forearms felt weaker, he exploded off the ropes with a massive right to the head. He threw it quick, easily sweeping his opponent's left out of the way and opening up an avenue for multiple blows. By the time the bell had again rung and the round had ended, he'd followed the blow to the jaw with one to the neck and three more to the body. Such round-ending combinations win points; more importantly---they win fights. Or at least boxing matches.

The fight was over. It had lasted less than ten seconds, could hardly even be called a fight. Ironic that lessons from a boxing coach were responsible for such a decisive victory. "It's all about the feet and the legs. The legs have to have strength and stamina. The feet have to be in the right position, the right place. It's all about the feet. And the legs." There were all the exercises, all the watched video. The stops in play closely scrutinized; any mistakes addressed despite the graininess of the recordings. The countless exercises.

A downward stomp to the instep; then a sideward kick to a knee, the blows to the neck and face almost superfluous. The threat was down; the sidewalk his. Whatever the intent had originally been; the would be assailant no longer had neither the breath nor the inclination to further pursue it. The damage inflicted and pain endured guaranteed several more minutes of incapacitation. The feet. The legs.

The seventh round was about to begin. The sixth had been his, or at least so he thought. They'd traded blows back and forth, neither getting much the better for the first two minutes. Then, near the center of the ring, he knew. His opponent was leaning on him! His opponent's legs were giving out. Not that he was no longer dangerous; by virtue of being nearly two decades younger he was still very much a threat. The arms were tiring; perhaps not yet tired enough. He was fast, could still launch that one "missile" that would mean lights out.

The fighter did not want to win by decision; did not want a victory based on points. His own legs had been weakening. He was at that point when you begin overemphasizing physical effort, when you drive your legs through the canvas as opposed to stepping upon it. You throw punches to the wall behind your opponent rather than to the back of their heads. You try to bury your arm up to the elbow with a body punch, not just the gloved hand.

He came out swinging. He wanted a soft target, didn't know yet if he had one. He went for the body; threw only a couple of jabs and then straight rights and hooks to the ribs and chest. Even landed that murderous left to the kidneys and liver. Halfway through the round he went upstairs.

Work had become scarce, especially with the closing of the warehouses on the riverfront. Globe Pickle and Trask Fish had provided work for his father and uncles before the war, for many whom had watched the timber industry wane and thin-soiled farms reduce their yields. He'd come after being released from his country's latest military adventure, a year and a half in rice fields and tropical jungles. The promise of carpentry had been part-time. Southern Cross had called in an even hundred new workers; informing them that by the week's end only ten would remain. Under his eldest brother's encouragement the three siblings had all survived, but the need for engineered trusses and pre-built walls had yet to explode as it would in the coming decade. Overtime was unheard of, shortened schedules the norm.

The middle son, he sent money home each week to his mother and the mother of his children. Every other week he made the journey himself, spent what time he could passing down the art of woodcraft to his boy, lent encouragement to what culinary and matronly skills his daughter had recently mastered under her mother's tutelage. Paychecks go just so far, even when bolstered by a Spartan life. Promises and apologies are stopgap measures, especially with the young. If his gift could not be that of his increased presence, the cedar this year would shade more than trinkets. His daughter would have the new Barbie doll, his son the air rifle. His wife the music box she'd mentioned in passing---twice.

    The right lead had caught him by surprise. His own right had simply grazed the younger man's shoulder as the opponent ducked towards him, the blow had both the drive from the twist of the torso and the added momentum of his weight coming forward as he closed. This latter movement allowed him to embrace the lithe assailant, to tie him up as he regained his wits. Tiny black specks darted amidst bursts of light as he tried to blink back his sight. Landing square on his chin, the blow had staggered him. Even now he felt the man slipping away, securing the distance to resume his assault. No longer confident of putting his man down, he covered up for a couple of breaths. Then again he hooked hard to the body; wicked punches thrown from close in, allowing his opponent neither breath nor space to complete his offensive. Enough wits returned for him to consider the irony of what had almost come about.

    His own breath raspy, he could hear as well as feel his struggles. Still, he pushed forward; he punished the ebony mass before him. Head down he drove the man to the ropes. Careful to not foul by butting; he continued the assault. Three rights and a left; two more lefts and then alternating right then left, right then left. His head buried against the other man's chest, he fought on. More conscious of the bell than was his opponent, he stepped away. He almost made his corner before he fell.

"That's all for a ten-round fight? By the time I pay corner men, locker fees and throw a couple of bucks to the towel guy, there's not going to be enough for what I need." Afraid his plea was falling on deaf ears, nonetheless he made it. He hadn't been in the ring for years, had only dropped by the old gym on Olive Street to see if there might be some weekend work for those times he did not go home. Was surprised how quickly the manager had been able to secure his current license. Pleased how easily the senses recalled the feel of the gloves over the taped hands; the muscles remembered the series of combinations as he shadowed for a moment to break a sweat and loosen up. He took note of the young black man glaring from across the hall. Eyes attempting to stare him down as he realized this was to be his opponent.

He'd been helped to the stool by one of the corner men he'd met only hours earlier. He felt like there were no longer bones running through his legs; imagined perhaps the same type of rope that surrounded the canvas square was now being utilized to connect his feet to his hips. They pulled out his shorts, removing even the restraining forces of elastic from encumbering his breathing. Forty seconds. Thirty, then fifteen. Somehow he answered the bell. He had to believe the dark windmill before him was just as tired; that the blows he was attempting to block were part of a 'last hurrah' and that he could quickly regain control of this fight.

This round and two more. As easily as this thought entered his head, he dismissed it; knowing his focus must be on the immediate. They were both circling. He in search of an opening; the other perhaps to burn up time. They closed, he again working the body; his opponent to tie him up. His confidence returning, along with his breath; he took a step back and set his feet. He was throwing his right when he realized he had not been properly set, his feet too close together and not under his shoulders as needed. He almost fell into the left hook. Friends later had to tell him of the two rights that followed. The same friends that wondered about the smile that commandeered a countenance only now regaining its senses.

"Tell you what" he'd heard suddenly, "I'll throw in an extra $50 for a knockout."

"You mean half a C-note if I knock the other guy out?" he'd inquired. The man was now even more motivated to win, more encouraged to somehow put this nubile young warrior down for the count.

"It's nearly Christmas" the promoter replied. *"Just so long as the crowd sees one of you unconscious, an extra fifty-dollars win or lose!!"*

The Deadline

Jud stared at the blank paper before him. At only seventeen, he was still the oldest child of his widowed Mom. Working at the local paper had been a blessing, allowing him to help considerably with household expenses while learning a trade. After all, the "first American" himself, the great Ben Franklin, had begun his march to fortune and fame working for a newspaper. Jud had advanced past the strenuous task of typesetting to some reporting duties, being sent often to one of the distant corners of Missouri's second largest county to gather the facts about circuit court proceedings and rural school board meetings.

This morning had held a new challenge, but as Jud considered it, a terrific opportunity. "Smiley" Smith, editor and owner of the paper, had just informed him that the typesetter needed two column inches for the front page, the much sought after "above the fold" position toward the top. Unlike his usual reports, here he'd even been promised a byline. He could barely contain his excitement at the beginning of the assignment, could not keep his mind from wandering to the reactions of his mother and siblings when he took wagon and team and delivered the papers later that evening, and presented them with the free copy that came with his salary.

But now, an hour later and his deadline rapidly approaching, Jud held pen in hand above a paper as completely devoid of words as it had been an hour ago. He could feel opportunity slipping away. What began as a chance to be noticed not only by the town and county, but possibly by the staff of the prestigious *St. Louis Post Dispatch* as well, was turning into a debacle of inaptitude and failure. At first he'd hoped to fill the space with prose to match the urgency of time. Something akin to the memo that should have reminded the skipper of the *Titanic* to stock binoculars for his lookouts, or perhaps a dispatch warning Leonidas that the Thespians had abandoned their post and he and his three-hundred Spartans were now exposed on their rear flank to the massive Persian war machine threatening all of Greece. But no such matters came to mind. He'd even contemplated citing some anecdote of wisdom from the lives of his family, but as his mother often reminded him, "The only thing your Uncle Jake can be held up for is as a bad example!"

He'd never known such unaccountable terror before. It was easy to understand being afraid when tracking a crippled bobcat into a canebrake, or uneasy about sealing up a hornet's nest after dark. But the feeling of impotence as the blankness of the paper seemed to challenge his very right to exist was uncanny. It was as if the light beige parchment were a portal into an abyss of inadequacy, a spectral program foreshadowing a life of little substance and few accomplishments.

He could feel the eyes of the typesetter on the back of his neck, could tell by the sound of wooden flats being moved that the larger headlines and masthead were finished and the smaller type were now being set. A door opening on the second floor above warned that the editor might very well be on his way down. Stepping onto the oak boarded sidewalk for a breath of fresh air and in hopes of some inspiration from the muses, Jud looked down the main street of his beloved town sitting above the river he so enjoyed. What happened next was to Jud somewhat akin to what the demolition of the *U.S.S. Maine* must have meant to the Hearst dynasty.

Bank President Tyler had just come out of his personal parking space in the first Ford Model A the town had seen, one the town folks had all been introduced to last fall; when Flossie Weber chose that exact time to cross the street leading Flo's Blue Baby, her Poland China sow that had taken a blue ribbon in Sedalia at last year's State Fair. Thirty seconds later Banker Tyler was in need of a new front axle and steering assembly, Flossie had the makings for Sunday's impromptu church barbecue, and Jud had his front-page filler.

The Pavilion

Todd had been a Level II Fire Service Instructor for several years, as well as having DOT/EMT certification. His HR training alone would land him innumerable jobs even without the fourteen years of experience in fire-fighting and safety rescue operations. So to find himself for the second Saturday in a row "volunteering" his time to build a makeshift shed on an isolated ridge in the poorest county of his state almost had him beside himself. As he attempted to place the board in his hand and realized, that once again, it had been cut incorrectly; he was jarred from his reflective mood.

"It's too short! I said 97 ½, this is 94 ½." Todd yelled down to Quinten, one of the three co-workers he'd been saddled with for more than a week. He'd taken to calling him "Dad", saying they were related by marriage. He'd worked with Quinten before; a tumultuous relationship at best. Though obviously possessing a certain skill set, he'd found the owner of a local construction company to be extremely opinionated and especially demanding. In fact a warm and caring person, he had trouble saying "Hello" without additional colorful descriptors. Usually it was done Quinten's way or considered wrong.

"You said an inch and a half short of eight feet! Pass it down and I'll re-cut it."

Todd didn't feel the need to explain that even if he had said "Short" when in fact he'd clearly stated it was to be an inch and a half longer than eight feet, the board was still cut wrong. "You'll need a new board. Make it 97 ½ inches." Todd no longer gave increments any smaller than ¼, realizing that at least part of his crew was completely befuddled by sixteenths and thirty-seconds.

"Whatever. This sorry excuse for a tape just has feet marks, not inches!"

"I guess instead of saying 'a heavy quarter' or 'light half', we'll just start saying 'a long three feet' or 'just shy of your own height.'" This was offered by Eric, the second of the crew. A retired college professor, he was trying to overcome his own fear of heights as they stood together on loosely placed 2x4's while screwing down purlins. Years of smoking a pipe had left him with limited lung function, so it was hard to be sure if his frequent hesitation was due to paralytic anxiety or shortness of breath.

Meanwhile, back on the ground, the drama continued. "You measure and mark it" Quinton was yelling to Kenneth, the third member of the crew. At this latest directive, both Todd and Eric turned their attention to the ground. Literally downstage. Kenneth pulled out his Stanley 25' tape but was in need of a pencil; Quinton being the "black hole" of carpenter pencils. He was constantly asking to borrow one and then tucking it away in one of his many pockets, from which they were seldom retrieved. So now Kenneth needed one of the previously borrowed scribing instruments; his supply depleted. So he was asking.

"Here's the thing" as television detective Monk would constantly say, Todd's memory skipping from reality to happy inner thoughts. He was still having trouble coming to pleasant terms with this work project. Kenneth could not ask in the typical sense. Surgery for throat cancer had left an inch wide hole in his lower neck and deprived him of voice. Fear of again going under the knife had left him only part way through reconstruction and the only sounds that emanated from the black abyss above his collar bone were a cross between a screech owl's mating call and the soundtrack from a 70's disco movie.

Todd started to toss down one of his, then had this sudden picture of the pencil snaking its way into Kenneth's throat via this unsealed artificial orifice. Fear of some alien invasion by wood chip or even sawdust was the reason Kenneth had not been chosen to do the actual cutting, for Quinton was still dealing with the repercussions of a road grader accident. A premature turn of an ignition switch had led to his being run over by the several ton machine. Despite a trauma center's best efforts, and in fairness he was alive; Quinton had quite limited use of his right arm and was still a bit shaky on his feet. The electric Dewalt circular saw he could manage, albeit with some difficulty. The Stihl chainsaw he used to cut the 6x6's had to be started by someone else, and then handed to him so the needed cut was "not as off the mark as if done by a blind hog" and the "barely fit for a starving termite" timber pillar ruined.

So, Todd tossed it to Quinton who subsequently dropped it and himself fell in his attempt to pick it up. This was the second day in a row he'd hit the ground hard. The swearing began, extreme in both volume and intricacy. Kenneth began to encourage the sexual behavior of the local nocturnal raptor population while augmenting his communication with wild gesturing. Always a demonstrative story teller, the flight of his hands and swirling of his arms had significantly increased since the surgery. Quinton's yells were now weaker, his breathing strained by his horizontal position. As Kenneth's attempted cries reached the stage when Bee Gees lyrics were expected any second; Todd and Eric started toward the ladder.

Though obviously uncomfortable in his effort to reach his feet from the unsecured plank to the top of the step ladder below, the sequence of egress had been previously established days before. "Do you have any medical training among all of those degrees?" Todd had asked the former professor.

"A little first aid, but that was years ago" Eric had replied.

Neither of the two was really at ease as they climbed from truss to truss, trying to attach the skeletal wooden assemblies to the support beams while making sure they were reasonably plumb and securely braced. Given the one could not risk ingesting a screw the hard way and the other was a bit unstable and basically one-armed, the reluctant firemen and the stamina challenged academic were all that were left. "Well, if one of must fall, it makes sense that the unbroken one should have some medical training. So you take the risks, I'll be the back-up plan. You know, the greater good and all that."

"Absolutely. The same logic behind elderly Eskimos getting on ice flows in the old days. They fed the polar bears and left more resources for the remaining members of the tribe. Wolves did much the same by feeding upon the weaker individuals in a herd of deer or caribou" Eric concurred.

"So if you see me falling, throwing yourself under me would be akin to the actions of our far Northern Native Americans?"

"Yes, in a way. On the other hand, if you feel yourself falling and push me down to create a softer landing spot; that makes you a wolf!"

"I can live with being a carnivore" decided Todd.

By the time Todd and Eric were on ground level, Kenneth had got Quinten to his feet and was again functionally miming the need for a writing instrument. The board measured, marked and cut; the four took lunch. That in and of itself was worth watching. Eric brought deer sausage, which he didn't eat because of health reasons; Quinton brought an apple to be healthy, but kept putting off eating it while daily diminishing Eric's supply of venison. Kenneth usually ran home, just a couple of miles from the concrete slab upon which they were building; still uncomfortable trying to eat while in the presence of others.

As Todd and Eric resumed their lofty labors, Quinton again took up his ongoing concern.

"I still say you need more bracing!" This had been the very vocal suggestion since the first set of posts had been raised. Two "A" braces were attached and then two more when the next set of posts were placed horizontally. The very first truss was braced to a nearby tree and then "X" bracing placed once a trio of trusses were up in the air. Lateral braces were placed along the bottom chords as well as the interior webbing. Literally hundreds of board feet of lumber had been used just to strengthen the structural integrity of the building, and still more was suggested (read demanded!).

"Dad", the term of affection now perhaps a bit more strained, "this building is reinforced beyond any wind, snow or even ice load it's going to ever be asked to endure."

Eric nodded his agreement, Kenneth even articulated some Hula style arm movements that seemed to indicate "big wind blow, building stands"---this to the orchestra backup for one of Andy Gibbs' early hits. Given the majority had sincerely expressed their belief that the building, a simple pavilion that was to be used probably once a year, was adequately reinforced; one might believe the issue had been put to rest. But they would be grossly underestimating the single mindedness of one Quinton Habslabber. The same Quinton Habslabber that had first effectively spanned a local creek with a bridge now nearing forty years old. The same Quinton Habslabber that took a broken down backhoe and single-axle dump truck and created a construction empire. Such a man does not acknowledge defeat easily. Especially when in his mind he is dealing with a trio of "inbred, uneducated and school learnt idiots."

"What about a tornado? You're telling me that if a tornado were to touch down on top of this, it'll all be just fine?" Quinton had that look of victory, the "top that" smirk he bestowed upon the vanquished.

Todd grimaced and began measuring. He didn't really regret the actions that had brought him to this point. Now officially a "whistleblower" he couldn't stand back and watch grant money be misused; money specified for equipment hijacked and appropriated for luxury hotels and extravagant vacations. True, smashing the Epson Power Point projector during the council meeting may have been somewhat over the top, so here he was. Forty hours of community service. Didn't sound like that bad of sentence at first, then he met the crew. True, he'd known them all before, they being both senior in age and residents in his home community. Even previously shared a few small projects. But this was different.

To start with, there was the absence of a plan. No, even worse, there seemed to be open disdain for a plan. For the planning process itself. Posts were not cut to length; necessary tools seldom brought to the site as needed. Then the speed at which they worked. They arrived on site each morning; he late afternoon or evening. Often the extent of their accomplishment was that they had eaten lunch. Of course there was the day they rebuilt two of the "A" braces. This entailed removing a half dozen screws, cutting three boards back in length, and replacing the six screws. They actually bragged about that day!

Much of the work had been easier than he'd speculated. Having your own construction business was a plus. The use of a telehandler (a forklift like vehicle with a telescoping forty-foot boom) made setting the trusses relatively simple. With the equipment taking the bulk of the load, straps on each end left two of them to simply guide the pre-formed structures into place. The fun part was the actual guiding.

Quinton had difficulty seeing the two standing on the walls. Since neither Todd nor Eric was extremely happy to be above ground, although just slightly more than head high; they were not prone to go out of their way to be seen by the operator. Kenneth became the relay man. He'd run from one side to the other to ascertain what movement was needed, then step more clearly into Quinton's view to begin physically directing the movement of the boom. Pointing with a single digit was not enough; arms were outstretched and the occasional foot raised. This often in cadence with the swaying truss.

Curiosity got the better of Todd one evening. He had to ask. Seated on one of the two trailers they brought each day, taking a much needed breather and water break, he addressed them. "We all know why I'm doing this." His fall from lawfulness had been quite public. "But what I want to know is why you're doing this? I mean, why is eating here so important to you? And why such a large pavilion?"

Todd's greatest shock had been saved until now. The three looked at him, and then looked at each other. Quinton raised his one good arm as he laughed, Kenneth gestured with both and wheezed— a hybrid sound of three quarter rhythm and mild screeching. Eric started to laugh, only began gasping due to a shortness of breath. This in turn led to more gyrations of Kenneth's arms and Quinton slapping Eric on the back with his one good hand. Finally he got it out.

"We never wanted this building. We don't eat here and we think the whole thing foolish! I guess we just needed something to do!"

The Legend of Ol' 95

"I still didn't find her," Billy responded sadly, fatigue mixed with frustration as he had just completed his third consecutive count of the boat yard.

"Well, it didn't just crawl away," responded Jerry, with equal frustration. Just last week he and his wife Lisa had counted all 105 of their watercraft and then seventeen year-old Billy Hesston had been assigned the task of filling out a chart documenting their condition, along with the status of their eight canoe trailers and all busses and vans. *Lost River Canoe Rental* was not only for sale and an accurate inventory necessary for any serious negotiations, but with Memorial Day weekend upon them, tourist season was about to go into full swing. All equipment would be needed to meet the weekend rush.

"I'll go back out and look again. I remember seeing it stacked at Pulltite last weekend and then it should have been part of that group we sent to Round Springs. I've checked all three gravel bars down there and we have no canoes. In fact, we have no canoes stacked anywhere off property." Although stacking canoes at some of the landings was a common practice before a big weekend, Billy knew that all canoes had been gathered for "the count" and that # 95 should be on the ground. It was obviously here last week when its condition had been assessed as the paperwork on the clipboard listed its condition as "Good." As a former government worker with no small degree of authority, Jerry was still the paperwork and drill and routine kind of owner/manager that Billy enjoyed working for, as technical school and career aspirations led him towards what he hoped would be better jobs ahead than canoe hostler.

"You don't think….." started Lisa as Jerry quickly cut her off.

"Don't start that nonsense around me!" Jerry bellowed. "Billy, go find that dad-blamed canoe!"

Billy was a smart young man and not insensitive to his boss's moods. Seconds later he'd grabbed his water bottle and was headed out across the field where all the equipment was stored. Besides, he knew where the conversation was headed and such speculation reminded him too much of the drunken talk of friends and family he'd had to endure as a child. His was a world of exactness and stability. Two years from now he hoped to be well on his way to becoming a Master Machinist, responsible for turning different pieces of metal into the integral parts of airplanes and engines, motors and mass transit. He wished to follow, no; lead the footsteps of those that helped Man master the elements. He had no desire to constrict his thinking to the ways of the past, when crops were planted by sign and stump water was as good of a pharmaceutical as one could hope for, appendages were removed on the family dinner table for lack of real medicine and "haunts" dictated which hills and hollows were traversed by hunters and root diggers. No, he'd just painstaking look again for Ol' 95; just as he'd done this time last year!

"Lisa, don't start" Jerry reiterated in his best simulation of Gleason in *The Honeymooners,* even shaking his fist to bolster the effect. "You know I don't want to hear that nonsense. We'll find it. It's out there somewhere!"

"Yes, I'm sure we will. We found it last year, didn't we? About this time, just after the holiday, we found it" Lisa concluded with the look of satisfaction one wears when they know they are right.

"It" was a seventeen-foot aluminum canoe, built by Osagian just a few short years after bankruptcy had forced the Lebanon watercraft manufacturer to reorganize and change its name from *Osage*. Many in the canoe business had long considered the southwest Missouri built craft the best bargain in the industry, its extra ribs and bracing making it much more durable for commercial use and at slightly more than $800 still quite affordable. Hostlers liked them for their balance and easy access to parts that did require some routine repair.

"It" bore National Park Service sticker number *16,* based on the most current NPS license; but retained the # 95 that had been painted on its bow and stern almost twenty-two years ago when Jerry and Lisa had expanded their business to 100 canoes and had purchased twenty new canoes just prior to the beginning of the 1984 summer season. Serial number GDF00604M78F could still be seen on its hull, though over two decades of commercial use had made it somewhat more difficult to read. As part of a large purchase, it had sold for much less than its newer counterparts today.

95's first two years with *Lost River* had been fairly uneventful. Somewhat resentful of the young weekenders who too often spilled beer into its cavity and used language it had only heard when riveters during the construction phase hit a miss-lick and marred the sides of a craft, 95 enjoyed the family floaters who came more often during the weekdays. She especially liked the children. They didn't litter, laughed more and were still in awe of the wonders of nature that the Ozark river systems had to offer. Besides, at a usually lighter weight they caused less damage when they drug across the shoals.

Jerry remembered back to the Memorial Day weekend of the previous season. The week before the big holiday they'd concluded their count and all craft were accounted for, including the new kayaks and the raft they'd had to trade two permits to run. Just prior to that Saturday morning they were one canoe short, # 95. Repeated searches had been to no avail, then three weeks later the Park Service had found it below Two Rivers, more than twenty miles downstream. No explanation, no equipment-just sitting there on a gravel bar. The years previous they'd been canoes short on occasion, but the lack of accurate records led to no definitive proof that 95 had been one of those out of place. They had recovered canoes down below Round Spring before, even below Two Rivers on at least one occasion.

"You can deny it all you want. I found the report last year and reread it. They were in #95 when they tipped. The boy made it to shore. The twelve year-old girl did not. They found her body in a log jam below the mouth of Court House Hollow." Lisa and Jerry had been through this before.

"I don't believe in superstitions and ghost stories. That accident happened almost twenty years ago. It was not our fault." Jerry, of course, had been deeply saddened when the fatality had occurred. Spring rains had turned the Current into a miniature version of the Mississippi, with swirling brown monsters throwing logs and other debris against the sides of bluffs and across bottomlands. The rise had occurred late at night and although efforts had been made, a few canoes scheduled for overnight trips had not been located. A family group of two had overrun Round Spring just after dark and their children's canoe had tipped over. The parents had suffered the nightmare of being unable to find them and having to finally take refuge on higher ground and then walk back up to Round Spring at dawn of the next day to report the accident. Due to the flood damage and confusion, it was several hours before they were finally reunited with their son mid-morning after locals found him wandering on the other side of the river. Only after the water subsided was the daughter's body found almost one week later. Death had robbed the once pink skin of its rosy glow and forever taken the light from the sky-blue eyes. Mud had discolored the shoulder length blond hair.

"I'm not saying it was anyone's fault. When we put that family on the water two days before there was not even a rain forecast, let alone any way of knowing what was coming." As a mother who herself had now dealt with the death of a child, the memory of the parent's faces as they first believed they had lost both their children and then later the mixture of guilt and relief when they found their son was alive but their daughter still missing was burned into a corner of her memory that she wished not to visit. At least not often, and never voluntarily.

"We'll speak of this no more. Billy will find the boat and that will be that!" Jerry knew also the heartache of losing a child, the mixture of exultation and sorrow as at each family gathering he rejoiced at the blessing of his remaining children and grandchildren and yet could not help long for what might have been had there not been the "empty plate at the table." He knew, too, the pain that such thoughts caused his wife. One more reason he did not enjoy these conversations.

95 was glad for the rain. It had made her job much less difficult. Not being a metallurgist, nor structural physicist, she could not explain the way she could travel along the ground. 95 became aware of the Skill three years ago when the onslaught of a silent voice invaded an evening's nap. She just knew that if she

concentrated hard enough her aluminum skin could crawl forward, albeit at a quite slow pace. The good news was that the observation skills of the average adult allowed her to begin her travels well before dark, different from as in the initial attempts when she first became aware of her newfound ability and waited for the cover of darkness to begin her travels. The actual navigation of the stream was much easier although she still could not find the strength to traverse back upstream.

Finally entering the river shortly after dusk, she again enjoyed the coolness of the spring fed water beneath her. Tonight there was just enough moon to cast the ripples of the shoals as ribbons of silver while still allowing the darkness of the woods to serve as silent backdrop for the glittering lights of the fireflies. She was well below Fire Hydrant Spring when she felt the presence of the Mother in her bow. There was still an aura of sadness about her, though she'd been part of this world for almost eleven years. Somehow time, even here, had its limitations and the Reunion; nor for that matter, the Search, had not taken place for the first eight years. Or at least eight years as canoes and living Man were restricted to count them.

They continued downstream, past where the Family had spent their last night as a complete unit. Snows and rains had destroyed the last vestiges of the little play shelter the Boy and the Girl had built. No signs remained of the evening's meal of hot dogs and cold pork-n-beans. Only a valiant effort by the father had got four "dogs" cooked before the rains had made their way downstream, having already begun the work of filling tributaries and dry creek beds to ultimately transform the now serene stream into a murky river of death. 95 could feel the thoughts of the Mother lighten as echoes of laughter protected by memory could once more be heard, as smiles again could be seen. At last they were there. At the Place. As was the Girl.

Her hair seemed more brilliant, far brighter than the moonlight should allow. The skin glowed with the health and vigor of youth. And the eyes. Two windows of blue that enabled one to see into a soul of happiness and excitement, awe and wonder. And peace. A beautiful "peace beyond understanding."

And as before, the words came, though unspoken.

"I love you, Daughter. I have always loved you."

"I love you, Mother. I will always love you." A smile lit the face of the Girl while these words went unsaid, while they were heard and understood. At this precise moment it seemed that there were suddenly more fireflies and their lights were brighter. That the moon now reflected off the very gravel floor of the river and traveled through its crystal waters back into the sky.

The sadness that accompanied this meeting two years ago was no longer present, the need to express sorrow and ask forgiveness no longer a part. Joy and happiness seemed to abound, and as with the moonlight, seemed to reflect off every surface on their journey back into the very heavens themselves. 95 had never felt such peace.

Somewhere in the next moments she was alone again, past the Place and with no one in the bow. She tried, just for the sake of trying, to turn and go upstream. It was no more in her ability to go back up river than to go back in time. Oh, that it were! She would again enjoy the simple beauty of the night and then before morning take rest on one of the less rocky gravel bars. She would be found and again returned to service, saving her skill for this most important of journeys, most solemn of holidays. Maybe she might occasionally use the Skill to escape the harsh sunlight, or the unpleasant company of those who "floated" but never became a part of the stream, those who come to visit but are never HERE.

"Billy, #95 is at Jerk Tail. One of the Williams boys towed it up from downstream. Guess it must have been slipped out in the current at evening and just somehow was not noticed all weekend" Jerry stated Tuesday as the crew came in for lunch. "Maybe someone camped out had it using it and then left it. Either way, go get it after you eat. Take the van."

"Sure. I'll just take a sandwich with me and go now. Jenny, I'll get the van if you'll bring me a sandwich and Gatorade."

As Billy took the sacked lunch a few minutes later, having gassed up the van for the two-hour trip, he could not help but ask,

"What do you make of all this, Jenny? You have a college education and a level head."

"I sure don't know. I was just a kid when it happened. The accident, you know. The only fatality Mom and Dad ever had, here or at the Camp. I just remember the woman crying when they found the Girl and her repeating over and over 'I didn't get to tell her I loved her. Today, I didn't get to tell her I loved her. Not today.'"

That night Lisa looked at the picture of her son. Her favorite where he was smiling so big and you could see the words still formed on his mouth, "I love you, Mom." She read the report again. "Children in *Lost River* canoe # 95 lost in muddy current, after dark when boat capsized. Son recovered following morning with minor bruises, suffering from exposure. Daughter's body recovered six days later." She remembered being with the parents when the Park Service confirmed they'd recovered the body. The anguish in the Mother's voice, the pain of words not spoken. She had corresponded with the Mother for some time and then the letters quit coming. She wondered if the Mother had found the peace that she deserved. Wondered if any Mother ever did.

The Ghost Mule

Calvin had just turned the chickens and completed most of his evening chores. After filling the wood box with kindling, he'd drawn fresh water from the well and then made sure the sleeping chickens' heads were facing inward and that their "dirty ends" were away from the well, and more importantly, away from their fresh water supply. Free-ranging chickens helped keep bugs from the yard and garden, but came with some maintenance. He'd already grained the horses in their stalls and milked the Guernsey and turned her back to pasture. At almost twelve, he felt good about the role he played on the Ozark homestead. His father was away building roads for the state and came home every other Sunday. He and his mother worked throughout the week to keep up the farm. Except for school, which was a three-mile horseback ride away, they worked almost side by side each day.

"Supper's on!" his mother called from the house. Winter was fast approaching and the road job his father worked would soon be over for the year. He relished his father's return and the days of hunting they would share. Still, he enjoyed these fall evenings when he and his mother shared a meal and recounted the day's events.

"Be there in a minute, Mom!" He saw why people called his mother pretty. Her yellow hair was tied back in a ponytail, the blue gingham ribbon matching the apron tied around her petite waist. He felt like his world lit up when she directed her blue eyes toward him with a smile. "Just going to put a little corn out down by the spring. Just in case." He'd been leaving a half-cup of corn on a partial stump every night for almost two weeks. Right after his father had left this last trip, he'd thought he'd seen a pale mule drinking from the spring. The next evening he had poured a small amount of corn on the top of the stump and the next morning it had been gone. He knew that the culprit may have been raccoons or even flying squirrels, but in his heart he believed it was the mule. The last few nights, as the new moon continued to fill out, he'd sat on the porch right before bedtime hoping to get a glimpse of the pale image.

After supper he'd excused himself from the table and went and sat at the far edge of the yard, hidden in the shadows but able to clearly view the stump and the pile of corn. With an almost full moon rising above the eastern ridge, Calvin first heard and then saw the mule approaching the stump. Appearing nearly as pale as the sycamore bark reflecting the moonlight, the mule stepped towards the stump and then gazed directly at where Calvin sat. Nodding as in a gesture of thanks, he ate the feed and then walked off.

"Mom! Mom! He came back! I saw him just now." Calvin was extremely excited about the encounter. He ran into the house as he proclaimed the success of his observation.

"Did you really get a good look at him?" his mother politely inquired, trying to match her son's enthusiasm. "He must like that you are feeding him."

The pale mule continued to come for the corn each evening. The night following Calvin's sighting it was seen again by both Calvin and his mom. A couple of days later the father returned home and was told about the new nocturnal visitor. At first he sat quietly at the supper table. Finally he spoke.

"I need to tell you what I've been through this past week. The second day I was back, one of the dynamite charges went off prematurely. I was knocked unconscious and lay in a little country hospital for over a week. During that time, doctors said it was touch and go. People on the job knew my name, but the few that knew I had family weren't sure how to contact you. All I know is that in my dreams, I kept getting on a mule. A pale mule, just like you described. Some days it would head towards the western mountain range. Other times we would head back towards home. This place. After the first couple of days the mule took me home every day. After about a week, I woke up. In the same room was another man whom had been injured in the same blast. He awoke the next day. When we started talking, we realized we'd had similar dreams. Same pale mule. Only his had repeatedly taken him up into the mountains. Mountains that he said were the most beautiful sight he'd ever seen. We both went to sleep that night. I dreamed the mule again brought me back here. The other guy died in his sleep."

Calvin and his mother just sat there quietly and continued to listen. Occasionally they glanced towards each other. At least once Calvin looked towards the stump by the spring. Momentarily distracted, he again focused on his father's words.

"An Indian, an old Cherokee, that served aiding the state surveyor heard about our dreams. He said that in his culture a white buffalo or antelope appeared to lead one to his final resting place. Maybe to us, the white mule served the same purpose. For whatever reason, the mule brought me home. Calvin, it may well have been because you were kind enough to feed it that my life was spared. You very well saved my life!"

Calvin could barely contain his joy at this last remark. Later, after supper was cleared away and all settled down for the night, Calvin himself dreamed again of the pale mule. Though Calvin had put out corn, the waning moon and cloud cover prevented any chance of seeing the animal. In his dream, the mule was bringing his father home.

Calvin arose early, but his father was already out and about. Seeing about chores, no doubt. Dressing as quickly as possible and putting on his boots, he ran outside to help and be by his father's side. Not finding him in the yard or by the barn, he even checked the well. Freshwater had yet to be drawn. No sounds came from the woodpile behind the cabin. Finally, he started down the road towards the spring. All at once an uneasy feeling had overtaken him. There in the spring branch lay his father, face down in less than a foot of water. Though a heavy fog had settled in their valley, Calvin could see the clear outline of the mule as it walked silently away. People said later the collapse was from the accident weeks ago, and that he'd passed out just long enough to drown. Calvin would always think different. He hadn't saved his father's life, but he, and the pale mule, had brought him home for one last visit.

Secrets of Horse Hollow

"You could hear the flesh crackling, the skin splitting," drawled Ed. "I reckon the boy had already passed out from the pain or maybe from inhaling so much smoke. Anyway, when we got there the tree had him pinned to the ground and he was just lying there. No more of the screams. Nothing but the smell of burning clothes, the woods burning, the leaves and rotten bark. And of course the smell and sounds of his flesh burning."

Here's where Ed leaned in towards the campfire and continued in almost a whisper. "His fingers had split open just like these hot dogs. Smelled like 'em too. Anybody got a bun ready?" Then he'd pull the hot dogs from the fire and start taking them from the long metal cooking forks, a sinister smile covering his face while he placed the food on a paper plate, knowing that soon the children would overcome their repulsion and partake of the food. Boy Scout leaders years ago had accepted the trade-off of Ed's help with his macabre sense of humor.

Ed had grown up in Horse Hollow, a rocky-sided hollow along the upper part of Jacks Fork River. Born in the forties, Ed had watched his parents struggle during hard times in the Ozarks, and listened to stories of decades of hardship survived by his family. He'd also heard of the resources that had aided his family in their struggles. The furs from raccoon and bobcat, the sale of dried ginseng root. Even the proceeds of the distillation of what corn could be grown in the less wooded mouth of the hollow and later processed in the craggy bluffs along the northern side of the head of the hollow.

Over the years, Ed had adopted stories from Horse Hollow. Some events he'd been witness to, others he'd heard time after time as a child and later retold as if he'd witnessed them himself. He was proud of his sense of history with the hollow, occasionally even boasting that he "knew all her secrets." He volunteered his time and woodcraft to constantly help pass on his skills and knowledge to children, never resisting the temptation to recite at least one of his stories. If a child mentioned that they were thirsty, he recalled the "summer so dry that the springs dried up and when working on the distant ridges, they'd turn rocks over and lick the dew from the underside." On a late evening hike that appeared in danger of becoming an overnight stay, some young men had been instructed that they later would probably be "robbing dead insects from spider webs" if they were to eat supper that night.

"These cookies are tough," complained young Rebecca, a member of a co-ed church group of young teen-agers. "I can barely chew them!" Ed smiled at the comment. Having been lost momentarily in reflection of adventures past, Ed could not now resist the chance to inject another of his stories into the lives of the unsuspecting.

"When I was growing up near the head of Horse Hollow, we were all poor. Didn't even know how poor we were. One winter it was exceptionally cold. Ponds were frozen over by mid-September. By Christmas, even the river had started freezing around the edges. The Howells lived even further up in a side hollow, the old man running one of the several stills that had operated there over the years. Not being a man of deliberate purpose, he traded a few green furs for the promise of summer corn and produced little product, with an even smaller amount making it to sale. By February, the family's stores were pretty low and Pa Howell had ventured into town to see about finding work in one of the stores or perhaps swap some woodcutting for supplies.

He left his wife and three youngest children; his oldest two boys being away at distant lumber camps. Being fairly content with the slow pace set by the patriarch of the family, the next few days each spent their time sitting near the stove and taking turns stoking the fire with more wood. When on the third day they ran out of fuel, each retreated to their corner of the two-room cabin and huddled beneath what blankets they could find to stay warm. Long story short, the old man finally returned after a week. He found his youngest, a little three-year old girl, curled up in a corner frozen to death, a stale biscuit in her hand. It had been too hard for the little girl to chew. The cookies aren't that bad, are they?"

The young people just sat there, the details and horror of the story still sinking in. Ed had painted the picture and they could all imagine the little girl shivering while trying to bite off enough nourishment to fuel her young body for another night. The mother and siblings withdrawn to their own thoughts, self-preservation and lethargy taking precedence over acts of concern. At ages where they still enjoyed the security and comfort of their parent's presence, especially during the darkness of night, they could only imagine what thoughts haunted the last moments of this young girl's life.

"You've quit chewing, honey. What's wrong?" Ed had to take one more stab at startling them. "That old hollow I call home has lots of such stories. Stories that need tellin'." Secrets too, Ed thought. Maybe it was time he shared more of the hollow's secrets.

"You all done here?" asked Chris. As youth minister for the group, he was appreciative of Ed's help but also aware of his reputation for shocking the youth he encountered. Anxious to call it a night, he'd been approaching the fire and heard the last of Ed's comments. The last thing he wanted was a parent calling about their child's nightmares after a church sponsored picnic. "Let's wrap it up guys. Grab your gear and let's assemble by the bus for a final prayer and then load up." Parents would soon be arriving back at the church building's parking lot to pick up their children. The drive back from the park would take a full ten minutes and he didn't like to be late. "Thanks for the fire and the help, Ed."

Ed nodded and went about securing the remnants of the bonfire. As he stared into the last of the coals, he remembered the expressions on the faces of the children, the look of almost horror on the girl chewing when he got to the part where the girl was found dead. He didn't necessarily enjoy their trauma, but took a certain amount of pride in being the "keeper of the flame," so to speak. At sixty-two, Ed was one of the last "old-timers" from his neck of the woods. He'd spent a lifetime learning of the old ways and times and believed it his mission to pass along such knowledge. This coming week he intended to again venture forth among the mixture of rocky bluffs and sinkholes that made up the head of Horse Hollow. He knew there were even more secrets to be found and told and readily accepted the responsibility.

The sun was now nearly straight overhead when he saw that what lay behind the ferns was more than shadow. The angle of the sunlight allowed for the viewing several feet into the crevice. Having wandered these woods for years, he was amazed that he'd not seen this entryway before, but understood how it could have been overlooked. The crack was quite thin and easily covered by the spreading foliage. Ed realized the extra weight he'd put on his once wiry body would now require the removal of his backpack. Wishing he'd brought a flashlight, and knowing he should bring back ropes and other safety equipment, a life of proud independence led him to lower himself into the crevice and begin his exploration.

Finding footholds only four and a half feet below the surface of the rock, Ed then crouched down to get a better look at his surroundings. Moving to one side to better allow the penetration of the sun's rays, Ed noticed what appeared to be the rusted remains of an eyebolt anchored into the surface of the rock. His mind began racing.

Could this be the entrance to the Lost Confederate Gold Mine? Long a topic in these hills, talk of the gold mine was legendary. Not a source of raw mineral, the mine was supposedly the hidden suppository for gold caches of the Confederate Army. Originally jewelry and other valuables had been hoarded for the ongoing war effort and then later gold bullion stolen from banks was hidden there as well.

This part of rural Missouri had seen some of the bitterest fighting during the Civil War as brothers of these Ozark counties were literally fighting brothers. Sometimes a narrow spring branch was all that separated households at war with each other. Too remote for successful military response to raiders, the region was torn by polarized loyalties and the ravages of that lawless element seeking only its own ends. Over the four years those that believed in the eventual rebuilding, if not victory, of the South continued to store gold in the hidden cave. Ancestors had insisted that its location was indeed in Horse Hollow.

Ed decided to crawl around near the perimeters of where the natural light illuminated the shadow's edge. His heart raced with the prospect that this indeed was the long lost reserve of Confederate resources. Just as he stooped to try to peer into the darkened space under a ledge, he felt his feet slip out from under him and found himself sliding down a timeworn limestone slope.

Cursing himself silently for his impetuous behavior, he came to rest against the side of a damp wall easily thirty feet below the hole he only minutes ago climbed down through. Catching his breath, he tried to stand and immediately felt his right knee give way. Pain felt like it shot from his foot to his hip. He tried yelling a few times, but believed that a wasted effort. Deciding to rest and think things through, he took a moment to reflect on his resources.

He had his pocketknife, an old Barlow he'd got years ago "dropping" knives, the Ozark custom of trading knives sight unseen until literally dropping the implement from your hand while simultaneously your trading partner did the same. He had little else in the way of survival equipment. He'd never suspected he would be even completely underground, convinced when he entered that he would be standing waist deep and perhaps look around for a few minutes. Talk about your "slippery slopes", he now found himself with a whole new set of challenges.

The rock he'd slid down was practically vertical. Slick to the touch, he was sure climbing back up would not be an option. Not at least without some assistance. After several minutes he decided the pain in his knee had subsided somewhat and it was time to use the remaining daylight to assess what further resources could be found in his new surroundings.

The sun was now going down and Ed realized he would soon be out of light. The knee had hurt more than he'd anticipated but yet he'd forced himself to continue to explore his surroundings. He had not even a thick shirt and nothing to serve as a pillow. As the last of his light disappeared he willed himself to lie down and try to rest. Every sound seemed magnified in the setting. Secure he'd seen nothing, no sign of life that could cause him harm or serve as a legitimate threat, he fell asleep.

As light crept into his new environment, he slowly opened his eyes and tried to stand. Trying to call out, he found his throat parched and dry despite the coolness of the surrounding air. Standing was more difficult than he'd imagined, the knee now quite stiff and sore. The way out still appeared unassailable. The wall glistened with dew that had settled on its face during the night, and even without this added barrier was far too steep the first dozen feet or so for a climb.

    Seeking to quench his thirst, he looked around for pockets of water, but to no avail. As the sun continued to rise, he felt the area beneath the crevice receiving the most light start to warm. Sensing opportunity perhaps slipping away, he sought water in his immediate surroundings and learned he must settle for what moisture remained on the underside of rocks that he could overturn and then quickly lick the underside. Being grateful for their smooth exterior, Ed continued to use his tongue to gather the liquid so essential for his survival.

Late afternoon found his leg beginning to swell and his knee completely stiff. He occasionally would pick up a large rock and gather the moisture from its underside, even though now his tongue was becoming somewhat raw from the practice. Although he'd tried not to focus on the rumbling in his belly, his growing hunger was becoming increasingly hard to ignore. It was during such unwanted contemplation that the sun struck the web at a far corner of his new abode.

Trying to push this new idea from his mind, he did notice the several larger moths caught in the spider's deadly trap, along with a grasshopper whose descent into this subterranean nightmare had turned fatal, despite its still attempting to move and final death throes to extract itself from its silky prison. Always priding himself in being someone that "could do what needed done," Ed worked his way around to the web and, leaving the spider the more gruesome looking of the morsels, he took his nourishment.

Daylight found another night gone by and his leg even stiffer and more painful. As the rising sun further illuminated what he now found himself referring to as "Dante's Retreat," he noticed red streaks running both directions from his knee. Taking moisture throughout the night had eased the soreness of his throat but the little shouting he could manage continued to prove useless. Ed decided that he must venture further into his new surroundings to find some other way or most hopefully some old timber that could be used to breach the foot of the wall and give him literally the "leg up" he needed to gain his freedom. When the sun reached a vantage point that directed light at least a little way into one recessed corner, he took off. Far too soon he was finding his way by feel, the remnants of light now completely gone from his sight. What in reality was less than seventy-two hours seemed like a week.

The three hours he'd limped and crawled was becoming a lifetime. He felt it! Wood, not rock. He had crawled into what was once a beam-supported room. He could now sense the ceiling was higher; the air no longer seemed so close. The first piece he'd encountered was small, less than a yard in length. Moments later he'd found another one, this one longer than himself. This may be all that he needed. Dragging himself the complete length of the timber, he tried to extricate the beam from where it lay.

Ed finally crawled to the lower side of the beam and pushed with all his strength. In making contact, he felt leather attachments and his feet touched even more wood below him. Deciding one of the other pieces may be easier to carry back to the wall, he crawled even further into the potential abyss. He felt along the side of some of these new timbers and his hand went across some kind of smooth surface seemingly bound in wire.

Closer examination revealed he'd stumbled upon an old lantern. Carefully picking it up, he realized it was not only intact but still had fuel in it. Even luckier, the lantern was of the style that had a built-in flint striker. Deciding to sit up and test his luck, he drew himself up behind the stack of timber and pumped pressure into the decades old fuel tank.

Suddenly he slid back, panic momentarily controlling his mind as memories of his last slip and its consequences flooded into his conscience. He found himself beneath at least two timbers, the globe of the lantern now broken. He lay back and again reviewed his options. Almost wishing he'd revisited the spider web, he felt hungry.

Drawing an end of the leather binding closer, he attempted to chew some nourishment from the dried out straps. After only a few brief attempts, he turned his attention to his apparent confinement. At least one of the timbers rested completely on his now injured leg and he felt nothing but pain when he tried to pull back. Deciding to attempt to light the lantern, hoping that the light would reveal more options as well as perhaps give him new hope, Ed struck the flint mechanism.

His world was an inferno! Apparently coal oil had leaked from the lantern onto the nearest timber and on the lower part of his pants leg. Miraculously the striker had worked. Unfortunately the event had precipitated disaster. Ed was trapped and on fire. The flames on the beams were spreading quickly and the heat was intense. The trapped leg was now literally cooking, from the burning cloth and the heat from the burning wood. The smell was almost as bad as the pain. Ed's last conscience thought was that of the sizzling flesh was somehow reminiscent of roasting hot dogs.

Some people take secrets to their graves; other secrets take people to their graves. Those passing through Horse Hollow that evening swore there was a sudden breeze that sounded like a sigh of relief.

A Casket's True Calling

Stephen Mason looked into the dark recesses of the old barn. A fixture already in disrepair when his parents first purchased the old farm almost two decades ago, the roof was rusting away and rotten timbers had long ago compromised the building's structural integrity. With the sun already behind the western ridge, little light came through the doors and windows, even less from the holes in the metal roof. Still, the gold color of the coffin's lid was visible.

Stephen had been cleaning out the remaining contents of the barn prior to its demolition. Having recently purchased the old farm from his parents who had returned to their native state of Texas, he was in the process of fixing up the old Missouri homestead. The deed had traced ownership back to before the logging days of the early 20th century. Margaret Thompson had been born in what was now a few remnants of rotted wood and sun bleached timbers that were once known far and wide as the Aunt Mag Place. Never marrying, she became famous for her knowledge of local herbs and abilities as a healer and a midwife.

Stephen was going to tear down the old dilapidated structure and build a new metal shed. He'd removed the few tools that were of value and planned on saving a couple of the original hand hewn timbers. What to do with the old coffin? He still remembered when his father had brought it home protruding from the trunk of their '57 Mercury coupe.

Seems his father had exceeded his authority at the radio station where he worked and sold some advertising on credit to a local funeral parlor. The Hooverish Republican station owner subsequently held the charges out of his father's check. The owner of the parlor, being neither a good businessman nor a bad man, felt obliged to Stephen's father and gave him the brand new coffin to settle his debt.

Nick Mason had accepted the portable final resting place as payment in full and considered their business concluded. Twenty feet of rope purchased from Dent Brothers Hardware and 27 miles later the coffin had been unloaded into the old barn. Neighbors being curious about the Masons and their seemingly strange ways were tempted to pry.

Remember, their arrival was in the days of electricity and cattle beginning their spread throughout the rural Ozarks. The Masons running horses instead of Herefords surprised many, as did the constant wearing of a knife and pistol as he roamed around his 300 acres. Even his constant walking instead of riding one of their many horses was cause for gossip. All it took was one of the Larsons seeing the coffin resting on the floor of the barn to begin a whole new round of speculation.

Before you could count the walnuts on one of the many trees that made up the yard fence, the local sheriff and one of his deputies arrived early one Saturday morning. Nick was on the porch having his traditional cup of coffee when he noticed two uniformed men prowling around the barn lot. Strapping on his .22 Ruger and Case's version of a Bowie knife, he walked out to meet them.

"Can I help you?" he'd asked.

"Not really. We're just looking around" was the sheriff's reply.

"Well, I figure there's a lot of land to be wandered around on here in the Ozarks. If you don't own some of your own, there's a state park right down the road. This land, though; it would be private property and not kept for the wanderings of under worked public servants."

Stephen, though a small child, had heard the story retold many times. The telling of it rang true, as Stephen had later witnessed countless times Nick's ability to insult and intimidate, all for no real reason. As told, the conversation started to go downhill but the look Stephen himself had seen far too many times told the sheriff that Nick Mason was not a man to be run over. Eventually Nick had explained the existence of the coffin, even offering names and phone numbers to assist in the verification of his story.

Both satisfied and unsettled, the law officers were content to leave the Mason place and the golden coffin still resting in the barn. A sense of pride made the sheriff open the coffin for inspection. Viewing only a pale yellow cloth interior, he went on his way.

Stephen's next recollection of the old coffin was walking down to the barn to feed horses as one of his childhood chores. Nick had discovered the receptacle had made a fine place to store grain.

Whole corn would be hauled down to the barn lot and then the 100-pound sacks emptied into the coffin. Nick and Stephen had discovered they could easily store over five hundred pounds. Stephen remembered thinking that it seemed only fitting that the bright yellow grain should have a bright gold storage container.

Of course, over the years the glow of the coffin faded and the cloth lining mildewed and decayed. Eventually the hinges became worn and the coffin began to leak. No longer suitable to store grain, the coffin remained unused for several years. Then one fall, Nick and his wife decided to decorate up big for Halloween. His kid sister had got married just a year ago on Halloween and he thought it would be a nice way to honor her new relationship and a neat thing to do for the kids.

Turning their front porch into a haunted house, what better thing than a coffin complete with candles on the lid. Kids went through the darkened porch, touching their hands to cold oatmeal that was to symbolize brains, picking up grapes that were the "eyes" of dead men. At last, they viewed a papier-mâché face inside the old musty coffin. Stephen and his siblings and their friends had enjoyed a great time that evening.

Stephen's next memory was one that should have invoked shame. Long before they returned to Texas, Nick and spouse had moved to town and Stephen had taken over the running of the farm. His siblings had gone on to college and to separate lives. Stephen had continued to farm, replacing the horses with cattle. He'd supplemented his farm income with work in the timber industry.

Inheriting just enough of his father's personality to make maintaining friends a trial, he'd had many different positions at several different companies. While working for T & G Lumber Company in northern Shannon County, he'd made the acquaintance of an edgerman named Earl. His better-known half-brother Cecil was well known for playing the guitar. Extremely talented, he was also known for playing left-handed. When first learning to play, an older sibling had refused to restring the guitar, so when Cecil played the bass string was at the top. The upside was that he could play anyone's guitar by just turning it around backwards.

Well, what Cecil was to the guitar, Earl was to an edger. When rough planks came off the headsaw, Earl flipped them onto the frame of the edger and, setting the second blade to the appropriate width, turned them into boards. It was the pride of a good edger operator that they could keep up with a fast headsawyer. At a lot of sawmills, the sawyer would have to occasionally shut down and file the saw to give the edgerman time to catch up, the fast pace having caused him to stack planks and slabs in the aisle to hurry and keep the off fall out of the way of the headsaw and carriage (that part that held the log and traveled back and forth across the face of the large circular saw). Earl was so competent in this hurried and dangerous position that he would not only hand roll cigarettes to smoke while working, but would frequently have three or four extras rolled and lined up on the frame of the edger, this serving as proof to the comfort margin between his performance and lagging behind.

Earl did have his Achilles' heel. Earl liked to drink. He drank cheap wine and a lot of it! His after hour's blackouts were notorious. One of the more memorable events was when he got off work, got drunk, but then woke up only a couple of hours later. Looking at his pocket watch he saw it was nearing 7:00 and assumed he'd slept all night and it was about time to go to work.

Living in an old shack close to the mill and owner's house, he came walking into their living room ready to go to work. Stephen happened to be visiting, and he and his boss decided to play along. Night and dark approaching, Earl, who thought it was morning, worried about the darkness of the sky. Stephen and Earl started up the old Case power plant, Earl all the time looking at the darkening sky and worrying about a coming storm. The boss finally took pity on the older man and called it quits, deciding that they "best not labor with a tornado possible." Earl returned home and went to bed, never aware that he'd "gained a day" in his somewhat tumulus life.

Taking advantage of one of his near comatose states, Stephen and one of the other workers found Earl passed out one evening when taking him a mess of fish. They hauled the coffin to the shack, placed Earl in it, placed a few candles on the lid and then started singing hymns loud enough to awake him. Trapped inside the coffin, arms pinned by the lower lid, Earl stirred in a panic. All his protests and questions were ignored while they talked about what a good man he had been and how he was going to be missed. Admittedly, the idea probably occurred to Stephen inspired by the *Andy Griffith* episode where Andy and Barney serenaded Otis, the town drunk.

Earl had started crying and yet Stephen and friends did not relent. Finally, the old man passed out again and they removed him from the coffin and replaced him in his bed. Neither Stephen nor his companions ever admitted their participation in what Earl believed was a horrific nightmare. They did, however, note a remarked decrease in his alcoholic intake for the next few weeks.

Stephen looked at the old coffin, considering its history and its many uses. Thinking about Earl still made him smile and still made him feel a little guilty. He'd lost track of the old man, didn't even know if he was still alive. Wondering what lying in a coffin felt like, Stephen suddenly felt the urge to crawl inside. Prying the coffin's two lids open, he lay inside. Still wondering what Earl must have felt, along with thinking about what he would do with the coffin, he reached up and pulled down the lower lid. Closing his eyes for a moment, he felt the rush of air as the upper lid fell closed. Whether a rat or his movement had upset the balance, he was not sure.

The smell got to him before the dark. Stephen didn't panic until he had tried unsuccessfully for a moment or so to find the inside latch. Then it hit him. The real, intended use of this metal container. He was lying in a sealed coffin in an all but deserted barn. He knew that shouting would be of no use. He had also heard the stories about victims being found inside coffins, their fingernails torn and bloody. He also knew that one did not die for lack of oxygen, but from the carbon dioxide poisoning from your own exhalations. None of this knowledge brought him any comfort. He knew that his own stupidity had brought him to this fate. He knew that he was now truly dreading the next few hours.

The Pie Supper

Sally retied the ribbon for the third time. There, the bow looked just right. Cutting off the extra lengths, she then used the scissors to curl both ends. Noting one of the pieces was well over a foot in length, she decided to wear it in her hair. Her decision on how to wear her hair was now made. Definitely a ponytail.

Her blue gingham dress would match the ribbons in her hair and securing her pie box. The earlier signing of her name on the bottom of the box now seemed superfluous, at least to the observant bidder. Still, it was the custom so that the young man willing to pay the highest price would be able to identify the lady who baked the pie and with whom he'd be eating.

She had hitched up the team to the wagon right before she'd begun getting ready. She remembered longingly the fun that pie suppers had always been when the whole family attended. At twenty-six she felt odd still being unmarried and knew that many of the still single boys were much younger and would most probably be looking to buy the attentions of the girls still in their teens. In the ten years since her parents had passed, a lot had happened. Somehow she had kept their small farm together, even increasing to almost half the number of their eighty acres now tillable. She had enlarged both their garden and small orchard. She'd even saved enough egg money to add a lean-to to the side of the barn. Here she was able to store extra hay for the livestock.

She had replaced the wagon, saving some of the hardware and lumber from the one that had slid from the edge of one of the mountain roads and made her mother and father to her younger sister when she herself was still a child. The first years had been hard and the box socials and pie suppers were a few of the community events that still made her laugh. Despite the fact that Rebecca's pies always sold for more and she was asked to dance far more early in the evening and by more suitors, (Ricky Joe once even had the gall to call her "the pretty sister"), such events had been a good deal of fun. She always enjoyed the music, and even though not the one known for her beauty, still received a lot of praise for her pies.

She knew she was pretty, in a way. Her father and mother had told her so, as well as a few would be suitors that found her common sense and work ethic greatly refreshing. It was just that Rebecca was so pretty! Her raven hair and dark eyes were a contrast to the sun colored yellow hair and blue eyes that Sally saw in herself whenever she faced the mirror.

Having placed her decorated pie box on her coats and wrapping it in the blanket she'd placed in the wagon for the cool ride home later that evening, Sally set out for the one-room school house where the pie supper was to be held. The building served as the school during the week, a church house on Sundays and even a municipal building whenever the circuit judge made his rounds. For events such as this evening's; desks were moved to the outer edges, a table was set up to hold the pies and room was made for the musicians. Like many such events, tonight's pie supper was to raise money for a neighbor in need. The Williams' home had burned scarcely a week ago and despite the fact that neighbors had already raised the walls to a new structure, there were many supplies still needed for a family with five children getting ready to face another Missouri winter.

As she walked the horses the last few yards she thought how beautiful the little building looked with light coming from all the windows. She could not help but think how excited Rebecca would be by now. Five winters ago a flu epidemic had taken her sister away even with the almost round the clock care she had tried to provide. A couple of tears formed at the corners of her eyes as she still remembered the lowering of the casket by the Jadwin brothers from down the hollow and their cousins from an adjoining county.

In fact, the oldest of the Williams children they were meeting here to help tonight had helped to dig the grave. She shuddered as she could still hear the first clods of earth hitting the pine casket as one of her uncles and then other neighbors and friends joined in closing the grave; the shoveling signaling an end to nineteen years of whom had been sibling and sometimes child to her. Rebecca had become engaged right after harvest and a spring wedding had been planned.

It was then that Sally quit going to events of all kinds. Tonight was to be her first social outing in half a decade. She was not even sure why she was attending this one. Over the years, she had sent pies to such functions. Had even made clothes for neighbors when similar tragedies had struck.

It probably started that afternoon when she had taken her pie from the cook stove and was thinking about which neighbor to send it with. Looking for something with which to decorate the box, she found the ribbon snagged on the back of her wagon. She'd rinsed off the dust and at that time noted its similarity in color to both the sky and the dress she'd made for church a few weeks past. As she looked out across the meadow in front of her place, the spring branch meandering through it and the promise of a clear night in the afternoon sky, she decided to go. "Today is a day to rejoice" the Bible had taught her, and He did not intend for her to just give up on living.

Entering the room, she returned smiles from many of her neighbors and friends from throughout the community. She even noticed several looks of pleasant surprise as she made note of a few faces strange to her. The Light boys were already tuning up their instruments, Dave on his Martin D28 and Roy on his prized Gibson 6 string banjo. Sally hoped that the Orchard brothers would be joining them later. She, like most of the Timber community, loved to hear Jimmy play the fiddle; and Rich was no slouch with his mandolin.

Placing her pie on the corner of the table, she couldn't help but compare her cardboard box with some of the fancier wooden and even metal pie boxes sitting there. Still, the ribbon seemed to set it off somewhat. All the boxes had some type of ornament---from metal designs to wildflowers picked fresh that evening. Some were painted, often with dyes found naturally in the hillsides. Almost as much care was put into the box as the pie itself. Here, she knew hers would take backseat to no one. She'd canned the peaches and the strawberries herself and knew from experience how tasty the combination to be.

She found a seat at one of the many desks as the numbers were being drawn on the floor in chalk for the cakewalk that would signal the start of the events. As her mind started to again wander, she heard old Ira Moss calling for silence, as the evening would begin with a prayer. He and his eldest son Phil would later be sharing the auctioneering duties. Though not professionally trained, their hilarious stunts and knowledge of almost everyone buying and baking pies provided a fun atmosphere and usually raised a lot of money considering the poor financial condition of most of Timber's residents.

The musicians played several favorites before providing the broken songs for the cakewalk. When the music abruptly stopped, participants stood on whichever number was nearest. Ira held his hat and let one of the children draw out a number denoting which "cakewalker" had won themselves a cake. At only a dime a turn, it was a fun manner in which to while away a little time with friends. A few unfinished songs and seven cakes later the actual auction began.

It seemed like an eternity and then again it seemed to happen all at once. The musicians were picking up their instruments, the Mosses were thanking everyone for their contributions and men were finding their "supper partners" for the evening. Her pie had sold. In fact, at $3.75, it had brought the second highest price of the evening. A tall, younger man had her box in hand and was headed her way. His had been one of the faces she did not recognize.

"Are you Miss Sally Bunch?" he asked softly.

"That would be me, sir. Thank you for the generous amount you put up for the Williams. They're really good people and I know that they will appreciate it. You do not have to eat with me if you'd rather not. The hour grows late and you are more than welcome to take the pie with you. As you can see, it is not an expensive box, so there would be no need to return it."

The words seemed to fly from her mouth once she started. Not sure of her nervousness, she did not want this handsome man to feel obligated. From his age and demeanor, she would not have been surprised to learn he had a family and home, so did not want to keep him.

"No, Miss Bunch. The real pleasure I seek is your company, though I have been told the pastry itself will not disappoint me. I'm glad you find the Williams good people, as they're family. I am Matt Williams, first cousin to your neighbor Jim. I'd come to the area for a rest and a visit. I've been clerking with Judge French out of St. Louis and heard many of his tales of this area, as well as received several letters from my cousin over the past few years. If I may have the honor, please let's eat."

Sally looked into his gentle face and noted the strength in his hands, despite their lack of calluses. She placed the lid of the box to the side as she began to serve them both, which was the custom. Ladies baked the pies and prepared the box. Gentlemen bought the pies and then in turn were served by the lady at the close of the evening. Some married couples whom had come together took their pies home. For others, it was a way to contribute to those in need, both emotionally and materialistically. Still others used the events to express their depth of interest or favor for a young lady. Not sure of Matt's intentions, other than to help his family; she caught him staring at the box lid and then at her.

"Do you mind if I ask a question? Where did you get that lovely ribbon?" he went on. As he waited for an answer, he could still see himself taking it from his pocket and sticking it on a crevice of a wagon when he'd first arrived at the community and stopped by the General Store. He'd helped his cousin load his wagon and then sat down on this wagon to rest. Feeling the length of ribbon he'd brought from St. Louis in his pocket, he did not wish to get it even dirtier as he knew he had another wagon to load. Matt could still hear Laura's voice as she informed him she was returning East and that the long blue ribbon from her bonnet was all of her that he would ever have. It had not even been a fight, just a separation of dreams from reality.

"I found it." Sally was answering. "It seems like when you need something nice and pretty in your life, God provides it!"

How very true, thought Matt, as he continued to savor perhaps the most delicious treat he'd ever held in his mouth. Or in his eyes.

A Petition Remembered

    Some things just stay with you, there being no good cure for their remembrance. Such was the plea I heard going on nearly two score of year ago. A simple, heartfelt request made by a man old enough to "have seen the elephant" as some old-timers are prone to say, and yet young enough to be remaining more focused on the fulfillment of dreams as the disposition of the dying. Still, considering the setting, the request did not seem that out of place at the time.

    "Dear God, please never allot me enough breaths to ever have to lay dirt on one of my own!"

    He'd bowed down on one knee and closed his eyes as he softly spoke these words. I had just climbed up out of what in a few more hours would be the final resting place for the vessel that had been Irvin Williams. Myself one of the youngest men that had gathered that morning to dig the grave, I was yet both old enough to swing a mattock through the red clay and elm roots of the old Lone Pine Cemetery and to have "answered the invitation" and been baptized in the Lord's spirit and in the spring chilled waters of Terrapin Creek, so I knew well that what we would be buryin' later that summer afternoon was no more than an empty container, the young Williams' spirit having begun its journey three days ago when his horse stumbled and threw him.

Mrs. Williams had held up well while his body was cleaned up, and even participated in his being dressed and laid out for visitors. As was the custom of residents of Chinquapin Hollow, the seventeen year old was laid out in the sitting room of the four-room sawed plank home. Family and close friends sat up with the body while neighbors from up and down the river came by to pay their respects.

Clem Williams, the boy's father, actually took it far harder. He had been the one that had directed his son to ride through the river bottom and cane brakes to try to find a young Jersey heifer due to have her first calf. Both full days he'd sat silently in the presence of his son's body, barely able to nod in recognition as friends and family came into his modest home, wanting to let them know they were hurting with them but unsure of what words could provide comfort at such a time.

Perhaps it was in the presence of these loving parents that had lost their only son, possibly while accepting the offered cold drink and selecting at least one of the proffered pastries so as to not offend, that John Brooks first began to appreciate the immensity of loss the Williams were suffering. He'd said his goodbyes and let the men folk outside know that he would be among those gathering at the graveyard three days hence to help with the digging.

John Brooks had been new to the hollow only five years prior to this tragedy. Unlike the Williams with whom a problem birth had left them with only the one child, John and Lita Beth Brooks had seven children. Five when they'd moved in and set up store as a blacksmith, two more in the first three years. Known for his strength and solemn nature, he never missed a prayer meeting or when the circuit preacher came around. Folks even remarked that on the rare occasion he was seen to suffer injury at his job, whether a misplaced hammer blow or errant piece of hot metal, he had never been heard to swear. One farmer later even remembered him actually saying a prayer of thanks for a mule kick that had torn hide and flesh from a lower leg, mentioning something about "opportunity for growth."

John doted on his three sons and four daughters. The two oldest boys spent time outside of school learning their father's trade. One daughter was fast becoming well esteemed as a seamstress. The remaining children helped their mother on their small piece of land, growing and canning vegetables and just keeping up chores. John's blacksmith shop was close to his house, so each day of the week he took the time to eat lunch with his wife and the two smallest who were not yet in school. Yes, John set great store in his young 'uns.

Which brings me back to that June morning. The grave was over half dug and I'd just finished severing a two-inch root that had cut across the northeast corner of the grave. I had dug it back a yonder past flush so that I could later get in there with that "L-shaped thing" to put the finishing touches on the grave. Claude Wilson always brought his old framing square and double-bit axe. The square he'd acquired in the city after the Great War when he'd carpentered up there for ne'er a decade. Ever since he'd returned home he brought that remnant from his city days to every grave digging at Lone Pine. Using it for guidance and with the efforts of his two-sided axe, Claude would actually make sure that each corner of the clay tomb was an exact 90 degrees. Twenty-years later he'd turned this duty over to me, but always brought the tools, the framing square now showing signs of sanded away rust and the axe always bright with a fresh edge from the grindstone.

    We'd laid out the grave shortly after daybreak mindful of the service being set for an hour after straight up noon. The opening had gone well and within a couple of hours we were a little past waist deep and hence more than halfway done in this solemn but cathartic chore. Graves in Lone Pine were not only square in construction and square with the world, allowing each casket pointing straight north and south with the rising sun coming up on a soul's left and retreating each evening to their right, they were all also a full six-feet deep. This being so often stated as the last thing we could do to honor their passing, we here around these parts were sure to take no shortcuts.

    When I climbed out it was my second break. Mr. Wilson and I had opened the ground and in the early going there was room for two working spades, a cousin of Irvin being the one to share the first of the digging. I'd re-entered when the Weber boys had got down two feet and some, they needing water and the chore calling for room for one to swing a mattock. At slightly more than six-feet and a third of another, I could bury either side of the versatile tool-either in the layers of hardpan that occasionally wound themselves among the otherwise red clay soil or to sever feeder roots from the numerous majestic giants that provided shade for the entombed and for those visiting. Even this morning it was obvious that there would be shade a' plenty for setting chairs up for the family at the graveside service.

At the corner aforenet the two stone pillars of the front gate stood the namesake of the plot of what we all considered the most sacred of ground. It was at the foot of this tree that John Brooks had rested upon his right knee and made the plea I still remember. His was not a position of restful repose, even though he had done more than his share of moving dirt, beginning with the removal of the first foot of the black loam that covered the red clay beneath. This he moved away to later cover the finished grave so that grass could be sown and flowers planted. The majority of the heavier clay he'd transported bucket by bucket to make room around the grave. But John was a man of great physical strength and hardly needed a grounded knee to rest.

No, this was a position of respect and submission. His supplication was humble and heartfelt. He, too, had served in the Great War, having had to lie about his lack of years to don the uniform and become part of the vast American Expedition at the tender age of fifteen. He said little about this time of his life, but those privileged to have sat at his table could not help but take note of the shadow box on the wall which displayed medals from both

France and the United States. The words came out clear and calm, sincere and unrehearsed. There was no break in the timbre of his voice, but his face was that of a fall sky before a storm, the colors solid and unmoving, tense with energy prior to the winds erupting in a display of mixed colors and emotions.

As he straightened back up, I thought for a moment he had caught me staring. The blue pools that were his eyes seemed even brighter than the cloudless sky overhead. His glance revealed no embarrassment, his expression more of an exclamation, a visual "Amen!" Anyone hearing this petition could have no doubt of its sincerity. I remember thinking at the time that for a moment, I saw no stirring of leaves, heard no singing of birds. Then everything was back as it had been. I took another drink from my canteen and climbed back into the hole. John Brooks joined me at the other end and we both seemed to dig with new resolve. Before we knew it, the lip of the ground was at eye level and Claude was handing me the axe and square to complete the job. Later that afternoon John and I again teamed up to finish closing the grave, the family leaving the immediate vicinity after first Clem Williams dropped in the obligatory first shovels of dirt on his son's casket. I remember noting that although the nine members of the Brook's family were all present, John had stayed distant during this part of the service.

Of course, all these things took on more significance a fortnight later, and to this day I wonder if the two events had not taken place so close together if the first would have stuck out so greatly in my mind. Perhaps they would. I still recall paying my respects once and being able to tell a widow that, although the passing of her sixty-eight year old husband was not easy, he had passed as he had requested. He had been found with two sticks of firewood in his arms, clutched to his lifeless chest as the result of a massive heart attack. I'd been able to let her know that this man had many years earlier actually told me that when his time came, he hoped to be cutting wood and that to meet his Lord with an armload of firewood would be an answer to his prayers.

But again, I've regressed. The afore mentioned memory stays with me, but without the power nor the frequency of the petition of John Brooks. The dead woodcutter was from a much more recent time in my life, and is a reminiscence that must compete with images from television sit-coms and movies of the week, the myriad of intrusions that accompanied electric lines invading the woods and fields of the Ozarks. An invasion in some respects no less aesthetically intrusive than a scratch in the polished surface of a freshly painted cabinet and no less culturally disturbing than spitting tobacco at a hymn singing.

John Brook's words came before I followed in his footsteps as once again Americans were called upon to save modern Europe from impending doom. His plea did not have to compete with those from the scared and dying I heard on another June morning in the swamps of the Merderet River or with the fervent prayers of the remnants of Company E of the 507th who later that night were shivering in hastily dug foxholes bordering the La Fiere Bridge and hoping the Germans did not attempt to retake this crucial position until they themselves were joined by re-enforcements from the 2nd Battalion due to arrive in the morning. That day had had its own form of digging, this type designed for survival rather than solace.

When I heard John Brooks speak so earnestly to our Heavenly Father that summer day, life for me was full of the dreams and hopes that dwell within the expectations of the young. Although I had been helping Mr. Wilson prepare the final resting places of friends and neighbors for several years, young Irvin Williams was only the third person of youth I had helped lay to rest, the Bunch children that died during the flu epidemic a few years back being the other two. The Williams boy had not shared my passion for hunting and fishing and the Bunch children had been far younger and had traveled in different circles, even given the small size of the entire world most of us called home. My two younger sisters were as healthy as Missouri mules and at the time I could not remember ever seeing either of my parents sick.

Death to me was what happened to the rabbits I caught in my snares and the raccoons Ol' Blue and I treed in the winter. Loss was when I found a trap sprung and a good bait taken with no critter having been caught. The passing of the elder among us was as natural to me as the yellowing of cornstalks in August, the falling of leaves in October. But there was something in Brooks' voice that tugged at me, pulling at something I could not describe but could definitely feel. Later, when I was to have learned that friends are not always loyal and love not always true, I would again hear the expression that "it feels like someone walked across my grave." At this emotionally unscathed point in my life, I had heard the expression but did not begin to understand it. If I had, I would have more likely believed I had witnessed a man stepping on his own.

Elizabeth was her name. Elizabeth Brooks. At eighteen she was already past when most of our women got married. The third child and first daughter in her family, her ability with a needle and thread was becoming legendary and almost every female in the county had something she had sewn. She dyed much of her own thread and was perhaps best known for her ability to recreate many of the wildflowers that thrived in our meadows and on our stream banks. She was not so much pretty as you would call handsome, her features running towards the plain but pleasant. Yellow hair fell below strong shoulders; a slim waist accented a full figure. The same clear, blue eyes possessed by her father shone from a tanned face, always smiling.

Her demise began with the errant stroke of a soiled needle. Blood poison was not diagnosed in time and then a botched attempt at amputation ended with a father feeling the grip on his hand slowly weaken, the daughter somehow smiling at him one more time as she shuddered then passed. Those present later reported the color drained from his face more quickly than from hers. He held her cooling hand for several minutes, the raging fever now gone from her unmoving body. None in the room tried to converse with him, most lost in their own sorrow and tears. Finally, he spoke. "You know, Lord, I've not been a man that asks for much, and I'll not be a man that is dilatory in his thanks. I do thank you for the almost score we shared our lives with this fair child, and I'll be thankin' you for the home in which she now peacefully resides."

    If you believe that we all have our limits, although they're probably further from the starting point than we often commonly might think, then you can understand why the blacksmith shop was closed the next three days and why John did not help with the digging of his daughter's grave. Those close to him reported he went frequently to the field in which his children had so often played, Holy Bible in hand and a Mason jar of sweet tea his companions. He sat upon the same log that had in years back been his support as he watched them at play, the same log Elizabeth rested upon later when it was she who watched the younger children search for four-leaf clovers and sheep sorrel in the spring and chased June bugs and dragonflies in the summer. It was said that late at night you could hear his sobbing literally for miles, even rumored that the morning of her planned burial the roosters could not be heard at three neighboring homesteads.

Many of us wondered how he would take it. He had slept on his own porch rather than share the room with her dead body. Though people offered to help sit-up with the family, these tasks were assumed by mother and siblings. The traditional visitations took place for two nights, complete with the offerings of food and drink; it was just that John Brooks himself was never present.

The morning of the internment the men gathered early to open the grave, the storm clouds that had moved in during the night now turning the summer sky a steel gray. The service was scheduled for early afternoon. Rain began to fall shortly before noon and what few hoses that could be found were being laid in the excavation in clay to begin a siphoning process, for the same red soil that allowed for such exact proportions and angles also made for a watertight receptacle.

John Brooks led his family to the gravesite, walking solemnly behind the six men carrying his beloved daughter to her earthen destiny. Protectively holding an umbrella above his sitting wife, John remained silent and resolute as a visiting parson began to read Romans 8: 37-38. A few moments later the speaking was over, the final prayer concluded, the "Amen" barely audible above the thunder in the background. As John reached for the shovel, one he himself had reinforced with a metal strap the length of the handle, a searing bolt dropped from the sky.

Ironically, the sun shone brightly the morning John was laid beside his daughter. The same men that had met early to dig the grave had also taken time to put that of the daughter in less disarray, it having suffered from being covered in both a pouring rain and amidst the confusion of a death at the culmination of the service. This was the third time in less than a month that Claude and I had met before sunrise to use the square and tape to lay out a grave, to drive the pegs and attach the grass string parameter that would define the digging.

As a kid growing up in a remote region of the Ozarks, I'd heard probably a hundred times "These things come in threes!" This was said relative to hailstorms, barn fires and deaths; virtually anything disruptive that we as mortals wished to impose upon some sense of order. Now the vantage point of maturity has allowed me to consider that, although it did not receive the same billing and its own Roman numeral, the conflict around the 38th Parallel made Korea the third in a series of differing global political philosophies resolving their conflicts on the battlefield. The eighteen funerals I've spoken at could be divided into groups of three, as could the six marriages I've performed.

Maybe there is some cosmic force that calls for significant events to be a part of some celestial trilogy. I'm not sure. But John

Brooks' death was not to keep order in the universe, nor was it a foolhardy mistake of a man that should have known well the conductive property of iron. I remember the look on his face, eyes closed, words solemnly spoken. He had asked to never "……have to lay dirt on one of my own!" His petition had been heard, and remembered, and not just by me.

Moonlight Memories

Brad waded slowly into the water's edge, careful to disturb the water as little as possible. Conscience of the many times his father had had to remind him that the larger fish must be stalked, he did not wish to disappoint. The full moon had allowed his lightless approach to the Joe Hole, the point where he would begin fishing upstream and finally exit Sinkin' Creek at the Forks, where Barren Creek joined in. The moonlight not only allowed him to traverse the stream hours before daylight, but also provided some of the most beautiful scenery to be had in the Ozarks. The stream was ribbons of silver as it rippled over the shoals and the dogwood flowers seemed to glow incandescent against the backdrop of woods and limestone bluffs.

The first cast of the black ½ ounce jitterbug was right into the shadows and the sputtering action of the retrieve lasted only a few seconds before it was rewarded by the crashing hit of the mature smallmouth. As he played the fish towards the bank he could almost hear his father starting to remind him to wet his hands so that the fish could be released unharmed. Gripping her by the lower lip and never raising her from the water, Brad could feel the slow satisfied nod of his father as he watched from behind to see that lessons taught throughout years of childhood were still followed. The twenty-inch female swam slowly away, full of eggs and content to return to her bed. The next three casts all had equal success; though none of the succeeding fish were of such size. Brad could still recall the words of his father, "The first cast after a careful stalk will catch your biggest fish in the hole. Make your stalk quiet, your first cast accurate!" Even in the clear predawn night he was not sure if the words he'd heard were from memory of a hundred times before or had just been spoken.

Over the next three hours, they worked their way upstream from one hole to another, not forgetting to try the small depressions behind a large rock or fallen tree trunk. Several more times his patience was rewarded with the exhilarating fight of a nice smallmouth. Never lifting them fully out of the water, he was still able to hold several up and admire the broad backs and deep bronze tones in the moon's brilliance.

At the last hole right below the Fork's, he'd taken his time gaining access. Afraid that perhaps he had made some noise, he waited a few moments again admiring the sights of the white dogwood flowers and the rising gray walls of Echo Bluff. As dawn was now approaching, the swallows could be seen against the sky, leaving their small cave dwellings and majestically searching the air for insects. About the time he was realizing the sun would be up in less than an hour and there would be many chores to do, he noticed a doe and her two fawns wading across the creek where they had been feeding on the watercress and drinking from the stream. Apparently he had "stealthed the hole" quite well and knew his father was smiling at his mastery of woods craft. Lessons learned and practiced.

Deciding, due to the approaching light, he would use his Rapala. He eased into position and made the cast. This time the underwater retrieve was met with a gentle tug and then a hard pull as he set the hook. The little Eagle Claw ultra-light his father had given him on his twelfth birthday bent hard as the battle was now pitched. Running downstream to gain the assistance of the current, this was a fish that had been fought before. As the drag on the Shimano slipped, the words from his father again could be heard, and again he was not sure if they were being recalled from memory or were again being softly spoken from near his side.

"Turn them back unhurt, son. That way you can catch them again. God gave us this stream and all that's in her, but she's ours to take care of. Turn them back. That's where the fun's to be had!"

This was an eighteen-inch male. There was no full belly, but lots of lean muscle. He'd fought hard and now was headed back to the shadows as Brad waded to shore and began the walk back down the ridge to the truck. He'd parked closer to his exit than his entry, knowing he'd be glad of the short rest before returning home to begin a day's work. First opening the left hand door of the old Chevy half-ton, a habit his father had started allowing as his health had digressed and these walks further took their toll, he finished by placing the rod behind the seat and closed the door. He could see the smile on his father's face. They'd had fun and "taken care of the creek."

"Good morning. Yes, son; a very good morning." His father's words were always so welcome, assuring if perhaps somewhat predictable. His presence as they drove home one of Brad's greatest comforts and enjoyments. His passing two years ago, at least for the moment, forgotten.

The Call of the ………….Couch?

Standing almost 26 inches high at the shoulder and weighing just over 70 pounds, Nichol's Big D was all blue tick coonhound. Daughter of Cedar Hill Jim, two-time UKC Nite Champion and granddaughter of Kelly's Country Boy, UKC Grand Champion; Big D truly housed the bloodline of champions. Even on the dam's side, her mother had as great of a heritage as well as the local distinction of being a fine "cat hound." Not only had Nichol's Midnight Dream (named for the predominance of black in her coloring) put many a bobcat up trees from the Jacks Fork river bottoms to the hills of the Irish Wilderness and the basins of the Sunk Lands, she had been brought in to run aground the last true mountain lion seen (and subsequently wounded) in Reynolds County.

Her lineage went back to the days when tree hounds were being bred for their endurance, nose and the quality of their voice. In the Appalachians and Smokey Mountains the deep throated voice of a hound at tree was not only entertaining but allowed the game to be located as the hunter may well have fallen out of hearing while traversing the numerous hills and hollows of this rough country. D had inherited the deep chest and accompanying voice that was sought after by coonhunters and her coat had the blue tick coloring named after the quilting pattern and just enough black splotches to exemplify what the breed should look like.

Calvin Nichols had raised hunting dogs with his father and uncles since he was large enough to carry buckets of water to the kennel. Although their packs had included July running hounds and even beagles and bassets for running rabbits, his fondest memories were of watching a young hound first bark treed. With their front legs on the side of the trunk and their eyes scanning the branches and sky overhead, their mouths wide open as they send their cries of triumph into the night; these were the visions that made him homesick.

Homesick and proud that he'd grown up in a small town where his family was well known for the quality of their hounds and he was affectionately known as a "hound man." He could still recall the first time Rounder had treed, although it was with other hounds and the game treed was a possum. Calvin could close his eyes and see Maggie beneath the small dogwood tree on the old Mag Place with the groundhog seeking refuge barely ten feet above the ground. He could remember drinking coffee for the first time when the two of them won their first local UKC hunt. Calvin was thirteen, Maggie three.

There were hundreds of dogs that came after these memories, as the sport grew into a business and Nichols' hounds were being shipped literally all over the nation. As his law career continued to take from his time spent outdoors, Calvin raised more and more running hounds and the tree dog line finally went by the wayside. Even his interactions with his dogs became almost businesslike.

They still all had names, but theirs was a job to perform and a service to provide. Their offspring products to be sold.

Finally, the inevitable had happened. Moving to better offices and brighter opportunities made the sustaining of a kennel and even a small pack impossible. More courses, more areas of expertise, more and higher billable hours. Bigger houses, newer and more expensive vehicles. More boats that saw too little of the water. No more the full cry of a dog treed or even on track. Every story has an ending, or at least another chapter. Differences over ethical responsibilities, frustrations over the downfall of the profession itself. Plain physical tiredness of the never ending hours and flowing of one week into another with no break from duties and deadlines.

Calvin had eventually moved back to the country, less than an hour's drive from his boyhood home. He now worked with his hands, renovating old buildings and crafting outdoor furniture with his wife, Shelly. He longed to hunt again and once more hear the echo of the voices of a pack of hounds as they pursued their quarry. He was sure that the primeval lust for the hunt was strong in his own veins as it had been in the hounds his family had shared these hills with for several generations.

He started with beagles. Miniature blue tick beagles. Three puppies that had just been weaned and he was sure would be found adorable by his wife. Shelly had grown up with bassets and these were close. They quickly worked their way into Shelly's heart and Calvin was emboldened to take the plunge. The pup he selected was six months old and had actually visited their home the last Thanksgiving while in the back of his uncle's truck as he stopped by to pass on holiday greetings. In fact, one of their little beagles, Miss Daisy, had been named after the larger canine because of the similarity of their coloring.

Big D, for Daisy, had grown quickly and Calvin knew by the fall that he would once again be part of "the hunt." As summer passed into fall his desire grew with the size of his hound. A bond had grown between the larger blue tick and the three beagles as they all four had begun to run rabbits that were plentiful in the three acres of the Nichols' gardens. Shelly found the "blue horde" constant companions as she tended the gardens and the small twenty acres of farm.

The "trouble" began in early August when the beagles seemed to be taking turns getting snake bit. As Shelly would bring them in to treat them, she and occasionally even Calvin would hold them in their laps while they recovered. Then, during the holidays nieces and nephews brought them in when they visited. Due to their small stature, the miniature beagles were the ideal size for the little children to play with. The next thing you know, the beagles were coming in after each hunt for "lap time." During all of these visits, Big D waited patiently outside on the porch, looking sad and forlorn as only the countenance of a hound can.

Just as the autumn chills were yet a few weeks away, the "event" took place. The "tuppies", as one of the younger nephews referred to them, were lying on the hardwood floors and on blankets on the sofa and D was looking through the windows as the sky darkened with a summer storm. Calvin had noted before D's anxiety during storms and now added to that was his self-imposed guilt about D not joining in at lap time. So, as the roads of life take many a twisted turn, Calvin was letting Big D inside and coaxing her to lie down on the couch. He sat there with her head in his lap assuring her that everything would be okay, much as the night he'd held one of the beagles when she'd been snake bit for the second time in as many weeks.

As friends and family would say, it went quickly downhill from there. D learned to lay quietly on the couch, after, of course, her customary inspection. She first circled the couch and inspected each piece of furniture, sniffed around the dining room table and then checked out the kitchen sink and countertops. A few raps from a rolled up newspaper on the nose did remind her not to place her feet on Shelly's counter, as her length of body would allow. She also learned tricks that Calvin, now calling himself the "Puppy Papa", took great pride in teaching her.

Big D learned to pay attention during the old movies on TCM. The "Papa" insisted she had grown fond of old westerns, especially those starring Jimmie Stewart. In fact, he was sure D liked any of the old Stewart movies, or anything else by Capra. He also taught Big D the pleasures of hot oatmeal raisin cookies, although he would continue to have to do the dunking the cookies in milk for her.

By the first snowfall D had a smooth routine. She would come in, circle the living room and then lay on her blanket in front of the fireplace. After sufficiently warmed, she would go stick her nose against the "Puppy Mama's" feet (Shelly had now been enlisted as another surrogate parent slash servant) and escort her into the kitchen to get the cookies started. She knew that when that "funny little bell" rang (the oven timer) it was time for her to take her place now on the couch. In a few moments Papa would dunk the round little puppy biscuits with the chewy centers in the creamy white water and then let her gobble them up. The beagles knew that they could gather below her great jowls and the "spillings" that dribbled to the floor provided some great snacks.

Come spring Big D was not yet treeing, although she did chase squirrels and birds away from the feeders and seemed to remain mystified when either left the ground and their scent just disappeared. She did continue to run rabbits with the beagles, making up for her inabilities in tight brush with her extra speed when a bunny took to the woods. She had now also mastered the skill of taking half of a cookie from the Papa's mouth while leaving the other half intact for the Papa to eat. Shelly and others were at first embarrassed for Calvin until the night he tried to teach her to use a straw. The results were bubbles and slobbers all over Calvin's shirt. When he just laughed, they realized it was far too late to be embarrassed. Or too late for any hope of regular decorum ever again in the Nichols' household.

Big D was found at the Papa's feet when he was writing his hunting column. She was in the garage when Calvin was working on his boat or re-spooling a fishing reel. She oversaw the cleaning of his guns and the sharpening of his broad heads and re-fletching of his arrows. She continued to run rabbits with the pack and even once bayed an armadillo when it had ventured too far into the yard. Calvin held out hopes that someday as she gazed heavenward wondering where the little furry thing and its scent had gone that she would note the nearness of a hickory or oak and maybe settle in on tree. His uncles continued to offer their derisive opinions about Calvin's "ruination of a fine huntin' dog", but Calvin had decided long ago that his relatives had too many opinions along with far too many old sayings!

Big D hunted with the beagles during the day and hunted on her own at night. She seemed to run everywhere she went and both Shelly and Calvin feared that if they did not occasionally pen her up she would hunt herself into poor health. Still, both of them enjoyed getting up early in the morning and seeing her curled up in front of the door on the front porch, guardian of all she surveyed. She was always quick to come in and help check on the status of breakfast. Eggs were her favorite as they produced more leftovers than French toast or oatmeal.

Calvin, perhaps giving in somewhat to the never-ending diatribe from family and friends, committed himself that spring to teaching Big D to tree. Daylight found him and her on the ridge behind their home sitting quietly (if you don't count sneezing and slobbering) downwind from a grove of white oak and hickory trees. As the squirrels came within view, off she bounded. Her deep-throated bawl echoed off the leaves and hills as she chased the little varmints out of sight. Sensory overload, Calvin decided, as he waited for D to circle back around. He'd need to find some way to get her to focus on one squirrel.

The next week, when the UPS truck pulled away, Calvin was ready to set in motion his new plan. Baiting the *Havahart* live trap with some of his wife's sunflower seed, he set about on Phase I of "The Plan." Later that morning, after emerging from the workshop where he and Shelly had been working on a cedar bench, Calvin found that he had indeed caught three squirrels, all young grays. Donning leather gloves he was able to release two into the woods and then placed the cage in the back of his truck and proceeded to the kennel to get Big D. Hauling them both to the back of his hay field he first released the third squirrel and then released Big D. She took off like she'd been shot from a rifle; her clear chop mouth indicating it was at first a sight race. She settled down into a bawl as she entered the woods and climbed the ridge behind their place. Soon she was out of hearing and Calvin hurried to catch up. Twenty minutes later he located her scurrying about beneath a large black oak. He approached the tree and began patting it on the trunk while encouraging D to bark. She looked up the tree, sniffed the trunk and then barked. A marvelous deep chop, more distinct and slower in rhythm than when she had run game by sight. It filled the head of the hollow with its sound as it filled Calvin's heart with joy. He let her continue to bark treed while he patted her and shouted encouragement.

Over the next few weeks Calvin and D entered the woods several more times, always at or near first light. She had now learned to separate one track from another and was treeing one squirrel after another. They would hunt for about an hour and usually tree two or three squirrels. At each tree Calvin would offer both verbal encouragement and then Iam's biscuits, as he would place her on a leash and lead her off. After returning home, he would let her hunt with the beagles for a couple of hours.

Big D was allowed to stay loose at nights most days, although occasionally Calvin would put her up if he was sure he was going to hunt the next morning. She remained the dutiful sentinel when allowed to sleep on the porch. Summer came on and as mornings became hotter the hunting trips became less frequent. The renovation of some camp facilities had grown into a Grounds Supervisor position and the time Calvin was spending with his hounds even further diminished. Once again management memos were being written, personnel policies drafted and adopted and budgets constructed and marketing strategies devised. Nights were spent focused on tomorrow's agenda as opposed to sitting on the porch wondering, which would come out first, the whippoorwills or the peep frogs. Big D was again looking through the glass at the Papa. Only the Papa was not looking back.

That fall, job offers concerning management had been forthcoming from the camp; he was already listed as part of the management team. His RV sat there as opposed to down on the river. The same line remained on his reels that had been there last spring. His boat remained in the shed, his hunting boots far back in the closet.

Coming home after dark he saw a rabbit run across the driveway just yards from the back door. Big D looked up and whined, then lay back down. Calvin went inside and then something seemed to call to him. Stepping out on the porch he felt the coming chill of an autumn night. Something stirred inside. He grabbed a flashlight and jacket and called to Shelly he'd be even later for supper. Kneeling beside Big D, he hugged her neck and whispered, "Let's go, girl!" Stepping quickly from the porch he led her to where he'd seen the rabbit. Her bawl led quickly to a chop that said, "I'm back. I'm back and on track! Try and keep up!"

After listening for a few moments Calvin stepped inside and informed Shelly they would be eating later. They went to the pen and released the puppies to join the race. They sat on the porch the next several hours listening to the race. Not unlike anxious parents,

Calvin and Shelly sat up until near midnight awaiting the arrival of the "tuppies" and, of course, Big D.

Over the next several days Calvin and Big D returned to the woods more often. The RV was home being packed for archery season, the job offers politely refused, the management team less one member. At the writing of this history, Calvin sits before the television watching *Mr. Smith Goes to Washington,* Big D's head in his lap while her eyes focus on Jimmy Stewart as he struggles to continue the filibuster near the end of the Capra classic. The Mama is in the kitchen making oatmeal raisin cookies, having had her feet nudged by D just moments before. True, the Papa would like to get Big D to again turn to squirrels rather than rabbits; but he has all winter to do so. Heck, he and Shelly have the rest of their lives!

The Intervention

My reluctance to be involved should have been understandable to those more familiar with me. Not only had I never before taken part in one, and despite the fact I had only heard of them on an episode of *Seinfeld* late one night when I couldn't go to sleep and the writers had decided Kramer wished to take part for the "possible fun of it"; the sheer volume, let alone depraved levels, of my vices tended to automatically exclude me from telling others how to live their lives. But the facts spoke for themselves. Daisy needed help. The debris from her latest early morning frolic still lay around the house.

Upon her predawn entry into the house, she had first trashed the couch, curling up on one end and leaving throw pillows scattered on the floor. Her characteristic drool was still visible drying on the green one, with the heaviest concentrations unfortunately on the lace edges. After finally awakening she had wandered into the hall bath. There, apparently undecided about a bath or shower, she utilized the same pitcher four-year old Gavin uses in bathing and proceeded to somehow dump water all over the bathroom floor, soaking the decorative hand towels as well as the bath mat. In her struggles to gain entry to the bathtub, she had even torn a corner of the shower curtain.

The signs that Daisy was growing increasingly spoiled had been there for some time. Not going off to bed when told. Spilling food on the floor and then playing with it as if the morsels of nutrition lovingly prepared by my wife were but toys to be batted across the hardwood floor of the dining room, a floor now covered with the scars of Daisy's disregard for house rules, frequently scampering through the house with unshod, muddy feet. Her passage into young adulthood had not seemed to help. The charming smile was still there. The knowledge that when she turned those big, brown eyes on you, you just had to say "Yes." She did not argue when reminded to do something. Her response was often as if she had not heard you, or that yes, your commands were important, just not quite as important as the task at which she was currently engaged.

My wife was right. An intervention was certainly called for, and soon. Otherwise the deed to the house and all the power that bestows might as well be signed over to an adolescent female usually more interested in preening herself than in contributing to the welfare of the rest of the household. The sooner we addressed the situation the better. The last straw should have been when during our annual Thanksgiving gathering she took over the couch in the living room and refused to take part in the after dinner conversation.

Yes, the time for an intervention had come. Something had to be done. Things needed to be said. Right now, Daisy was reclined on some pillows on the floor watching a rerun of *Broadcast News,* having long been an Albert Brooks fan. Her realization that I was more comfortable listening to classical music while trying to write apparently meant little to her, the distraction of the television not her concern. There was no question something had to be said. The question was, what do you say to a 75 pound blue tick hound that has taken over your home?

Oh, What A Name!

They had just discussed completion of the child's homework when the ten-year old changed the subject.

"Dad, why are there not more Terry's in the world? I mean there are several Smiths in school, two different sets of Jones just in my class. I looked in the phone book and we're the only Terry's. Why?"

The father had known he would have this subject to broach someday, actually had looked forward to it. Was in fact quite proud of the situation, the legacy of his family name. Eagerly he responded.

"That's a mighty fine question, young man. A mighty fine question. And there's a mighty fine answer." Smiling, he continued.

"In the beginning, there was just one surname for everyone. Only one last name for all the families in the entire world. And son, that name I am proud to say was 'Terry.'"

The boy's eyes widened in wonder. His cherubic face began to glow with shared pride. Then the young countenance displayed confusion, just a bit. And growing curiosity.

"Dad, what happened? How come they're not all named Terry now?"

"Well, in the very beginning, Man was without sin. Without sin and all named Terry. Over the years, the centuries, as a family would sin they had to change their name." Smiling at the story he himself had been told as a young man, he started to leave the room. Once more, his young son spoke.

"Is that why Grandpa spelled his name Terrey with an extra 'e' and we dropped it?"

Great Expectations—Ozark Style

Kelly had called Bob in advance, let him know he'd be gigging later that evening. Since he was leaving town for the following two days, he'd not have time to cook them for him and the other neighbors as was usual. He'd clean them at the river and deliver them about 8:00 PM. Bob was agreed, and as typical, quite appreciative.

The neighbor's had been sharing fish fries for a decade. Kelly loved to fish, and was fairly good at it. Bob loved to eat fish, and was real good at it! From spring crappie to summer bass, fall walleye and winter suckers; they'd shared them all. Generally Kelly cooked them at his home, but on occasion just delivered raw, cleaned fish to Bob's home.

Kelly was breaking in new giggers. A young couple recently married that did not have their own boat. Eager and friendly, Solomon and Jodi's skill had yet to match their enthusiasm. As in past evenings, they'd met and launched the boat before dusk. Had run downstream and cooked hot dogs prior to dark and then gigged back upstream under the halogen lights.

A good time was had by all, the young couple seeing several fish. Harvesting a few. After the boat was back at the launching site, having run the larger holes at least twice, the fish were cleaned. To make cooking easier, Kelly went ahead and filleted them. Even made the required parallel cuts down to skin so that the hot grease would crystalize the tiny bones.

He'd bid the kids goodnight, dropped his boat off at his house and wound the mile and a half up to his neighbor's home. Saw their porch light; knew they were expecting him. Pulled up and grabbed the fresh fillets. Saw the problem.

More a discrepancy than a problem. In his one hand he held a small container of eight modest fillets. In her two hands Bob's wife held a three-gallon dish pan.

The Handshake

"Put 'er there, young man." The larger than life driver extended his beefy hand to the young man.

The nine year old boy reluctantly reached out and watched as his now seemingly tiny hand was swallowed; relieved when he felt firm but not crushing pressure. Kept staring at the end of his arm and was visibly anxious to retrieve it.

"That's not a handshake" he was told by the gentle giant. Greg was a large man; great of both stature and heart. He was quick with a smile for stranger and friend alike, had worked all his life and was now building up a small oil business. Loved what some might refer to as the three "c's", Christ, capitalism and children.

"You look a man right in the eye when you shake his hand. Show him you've nothing to hide. Grasp it firm; you let him know there's a man at the end of that arm."

Gavin smiled, believing he'd endured this ordeal and life would move on. "Yes, sir" he replied politely. He began to walk away.

"Hold on now" Greg continued. "We're going to do this thing 'til we get it right. Put 'er there!" This time Gavin looked him in the eye, squeezed a bit more firmly.

After about ten minutes and a half-dozen rehearsals, the owner/operator said his goodbyes and resumed his route. His final handshake had gone well. They'd even practiced introductions.

"There's a lot of truth to that old saying about having just one chance to make a first impression. Make a good one." The young boy listened as the lesson continued and then ended.

As the truck started down the driveway, Gavin could be heard quietly asking. "But when do we practice goodbyes?"

Rainbow Springs

Glen believed in the teachings of his childhood. Though his degree of sanguinity was far from full, Welsh blood obviously flowed through his veins. Lineage going back to the Iberian Peninsula was apparent in the swarthy skin, thick black hair and almost ebony eyes. What outcrosses that had occurred included mixing with other Celtic clans in southern Ireland and then in coming to America, descendants of the Osage tribe. Though environment certainly played a significant part, and he had indeed learned from a father, uncles and a grandfather that all lived more in the woods than in their respective homes; Glen had seemed part of the earth since birth.

He could course a running hound and then outrun a deer to a crossing when barely a teenager. He swam before he walked, and walked early. Friends said that he could hear clouds moving overhead, feel the steps of a mature buck slipping through a canebrake or sense a trout begin to rise to a fly. Could even smell mushrooms emerging from the soil.

Like many from rural Shannon County, he'd sought work in St. Louis. A good deal of strength and endurance made him suited for construction. A natural fearlessness led to him working high steel. Fourteen in 1945, he'd missed the war in Europe but at only sixteen had a faked ID and was part of the postwar boom.

At nineteen he joined the Army and was part of the 3rd Battalion's 34th Infantry that got driven from Choson and lost more than two-thirds of their men as they finally regrouped at the Kum River. Shrapnel injuries a year later sent him home from Korea and back to the Ozarks.

Glen got a job working for Bufford Lewis at his grocery and gas station at the foot of Spring Valley Hill. Stayed in one of Patterson's cabins for a while before building his own cabin near the Mouth of Sinking Creek. Though he worked on other's cars, he walked or rode a mule most places he went.

Glen did a little guide work for Walter Carr, continued to work for Lewis—mainly on work trucks and tractors. He found he had a knack for fixing them. Independent Stave was sending him a lot of business.

At twenty nine he'd had his heart broken twice. When his grandfather died he was on a four day float to Van Buren. The heart attack had occurred the morning after he'd left Pulltite; the burial while he was camped at Gravel Springs. The other time was after paying fourteen dollars for a girl's pie at a Union Hill School fundraiser.

He'd first met the girl at Dance Hall Cave back on Blair's Creek. Auburn hair and green eyes. Skin the color of fresh milk. They'd danced far past midnight. Even shared a tin cup of some of the local shine being distributed.

As tradition held, she served him the pie; sat and ate with him. Refused an offer to be taken home, though he'd borrowed and cleaned up a '39 Ford coupe just for the occasion. He'd heard later she was interested in another boy. Another boy who had warned her of the rough edges of Glen and his family.

It was spring and he knew he should be looking forward to warmer weather. To the renewal of life played out each year in the Ozark woodland. The green appearing at the ends of dogwood twigs. The eventual four-leafed ivory flowers, the redbuds that would add their accent of magenta pink. The mating calls of turkey blending with the art show that was the rays from a rising sun.

Somehow he felt lost. The reassuring connection he'd enjoyed all his life seemed to be slipping away. He missed a striking fish; was wet before he sensed an oncoming rain. Mistook the barking of a fox for the grunting of a badger. Had to look twice at bear scat to know upon what it had recently feasted. Glen felt something important within him was withering and at risk of dying.

At one time or another he'd seen nearly every active spring on Upper Current River, had drunk from the majority. Had actually discovered a few that came up midstream, such as the one below Fire Hydrant Spring. The almost unperceivable swirling sand on the river's floor their only indicator of location. Today he searched for one which he'd never seen. One that few even knew existed.

Glen had first heard of it from his grandfather; then later from an aunt. She had sought it out after losing a child, a little girl who fell from the wagon while the family was harvesting corn. A crushed leg developed a blood clot and the child was gone in just hours from the accident. The aunt's soul began to wither along with the damaged appendage.

Within the first month the other children were being neglected. Clothes not washed; bathes not taken. What they might have missed most was the telling of bedtime stories, always accompanied with evening prayers. If pushed to it, they would have admitted the quality of the table fare had fell off a might. It was then her uncle, Glen's grandfather, had told her of the spring. She'd later told Glen.

His grandfather had originally told him of the spring. The older relative and mentor had visited the spring upon his return from Europe in 1918. He'd made it home by Christmas, sporting the limp Glen would always remember. What the young boy didn't know was exactly how his grandfather had received it.

The Battle of Belleau Wood, where the Germans had pushed back after losses at Verdun and Somme, saw some of the bitterest fighting of the Great War as it was then known. The Marines his infantry unit had served beside had taken heavy casualties. The young soldier had faced artillery barrages for nearly twelve straight hours dragging wounded back to safety and first aid. What would drive him to trek through a half foot of snow that Missouri winter was not the dead. Nor the dying. It was the handful of living that were rifling the corpses for whatever they could find. That, and the fact he did nothing to stop them.

    Glen knew he was not merely the third generation to seek the magical waters. The spring's legendary powers to fill whatever specific void someone suffered were whispered of in remote places. Celts had spoken of it for centuries. Irish immigrants had carried the tales from the Old Country. There was talk of such waters in County Cork, in the ancient province of Munster near the village of Rylane Cross at the foothills of the Boggeragh Mountains. The Irish spring may very well have been the source of later folklore.

    Glen had crossed White Oak Flats, traversed Basket Hollow and was now on the ridge that if followed far enough would take one into the Sunklands. The rain had dwindled to a fine mist and this was fast giving way to an emerging sun. It was a short moment later he saw it.

    The northern end of origin was still lost in a growing fog bank rising from the river bottom, but the southern haunch of the rainbow terminated in a rocky crag less than a quarter mile away, slightly aforenet of his present position. Silently offering up a prayer to his Creator, he moved forward.

    For a moment the crystal like liquid reflected the colors of his roadmap. As advised, he cupped his hand and raised the water to his lips, all the while keeping his eyes focused on the slowly dissipating colors. The distinction between the red and orange becoming more obscure. He kept staring upward as he continued to drink.

As the last of the indigo and blue merged into the now steel gray of the darkening sky, the rain began again. Softly, with the subtleness of some countenance barely changing expression. It was several minutes before he realized the spring was no longer running. That the water now in his cupped hand was coming from the rain.

He started walking back towards the river, knowing after that two miles he had nearly seven more before being at his cabin. He wondered if it had made a difference. And then he smelled them. The morels that would later appear overnight. The woodland delicacy that in its golden splendor so well graces skillets throughout the Ozarks. His step lightened at the thought.

A River's Cries

Judy edged the craft known as a Current River Jonboat from the bank and started downstream. The wooden vessel which had a rake both fore and aft steered easily over the shoals of the spring fed waters, its draft mid-craft still quite shallow. Her son had mounted the 9.8 horsepower Mercury outboard to the stern just in case, but by nature these boats were known for "finding the current" and typically required little steering save for the most trying of chutes.

This day Judy did not wish to run the motor unless for some reason she needed to head back upstream. She looked forward to the peace and quiet of the early fall day. Often, throughout the float, she would close her eyes and recline against the back of the cane-bottomed guide chair in which she sat. She would do this briefly at the start of a hole, giving herself time to listen for the sounds of the river before having to arise and prepare for the next shoal. Sounds she'd cherished since childhood.

What she noticed first was what she did not hear. As she drifted past Welch Cave there were no sounds of fishing at the Trout Club. There had been no sounds from the sanitarium for years, but the cabins had remained busy with visiting fly fishermen until the takeover.

Though a pretty day with virtually no wind, the verses of songs such as *The Old Rugged Cross* and *Shine, Jesus, Shine* were not to be heard wafting down from the overlooking ridge. Neither were they echoing up from below the ferry where loved ones had long gathered for the baptism of friends and family.

The ferry was still in operation, but the store had changed dramatically. No longer was it a Post Office, though it had been for decades, with numerous of her family serving the position of Post Mistress as had her own mother going back to a grandfather that served as Post Master. No longer could you get a haircut, though her father's scissors and shears were still in the family. People no longer gathered around a pot-bellied stove and shared stories of community "goings and doings."

The stove had long since been removed, as had the telephone station which had been manned fulltime for several years. Someone had to be there to manually switch the cables connecting the different callers. Livestock and grain prices were not speculated about; neither was locally manufactured moonshine distributed by her Uncle Doc.

The school bell did not ring out to call students back from recess. The dusting of erasers was not heard, nor was the recitation of spelling words or the excited cries of children competing in math ciphers. There were no cries from an auctioneer as bids were solicited at a pie supper to raise money for textbooks or to assist some family in dire need. In fact, the structure itself was torn down. As were most of the homes where people used to come out on a porch and visit with passing floaters.

Greetings no longer rang out announcing cookies coming out of the oven or cold lemonade just freshly squeezed. A watermelon cooled ready to share, or a letter to be read aloud to friends.

The Akers Cemetery was still intact, but concerns about it being to a degree under Federal stewardship had changed things. Her very own parents had chosen to be buried elsewhere because of concerns that this cemetery might very well suffer the fates of others. The Purcell Cemetery across from Cave Springs was no longer recognizable, despite the fact there were war veterans buried there.

Passing Cave Springs there was no laughter from picnickers by the mouth of the cave. No melons splashing as they are placed in a burlap bag and dropped into the cold spring water to be cooled. No "Hello!" from her Aunt Beanie across the river.

As she rounded the old Blackwell Place, there were no sounds from the one time farming operation. There were at least still camping sounds from Pulltite. The campground that her parents had started at Akers had been closed almost twenty years.

As she climbed out of the craft that had been in the family for many years, the type of boat that had been named for the river on which it was first designed; her thoughts remained on what she had not heard. On sounds not heard for years, decades. But what had she heard that day?

She remembered the night a US Marshall had served the papers that would take their family home. Papers similar to those being served up and down the river. She remembered feeling as if someone had died. The tears, even from adults. That's what she'd heard today. The cries of a river.

Author's Notes

Some of the previous stories were based on my experiences and thinly veiled. Others inspired by those past experiences and a few total creations of my imagination. A few were based on stories I heard as a child. I believe they are all geographically and historically accurate. Following is a synopsis of each, with what I hope are helpful commentary provided so there may exist a clear understanding of what is fact and what is fiction.

I truly hope you have enjoyed this book and that it has in some way inspired you to visit the areas described. Even more, to learn more of the cultures represented. Please look for more upcoming works, including *The Commentary Boat*. It is the first in a trilogy of the Ozarks beginning in 1967, with a strong Christian teenage girl as the protagonist. Now for the comments.

A Cargo Predestined

Highway 19 was built by horse drawn equipment and Round Spring Bridge was dedicated in 1924. These better roads led to the creation of Round Spring State Park in 1934; though private recreational facilities were already maintained there.

I combined two stories that I'd heard from my childhood; both presented as true accounts.

For those that might access today's resources and believe Toil and Trouble could not have been that big, please note that at the

1904 World's Fair in St. Louis they had specific classes for Mules and Mule Pairs in excess of 16 hands. A mule mare named Lil was shown by J. P. Wilson of Wellsville, Missouri. Lil stood 17 hands and weighed 1560 pounds. In *Macbeth* the witches did not have names. The three witches were referred to as the Weird Sisters. The mule's names came from one of their incantations as written by Shakespeare. Though Potts Freight is a creation, there is a Potts Hole on both Current River and Sinkin' Creek where there is also the remnants of the Potts Place.

Blood Red

All of the killings were fictitious, though the settings all historically accurate. The mill was mistakenly pink for a while, I believe in the early 1990's. It was painted white with green trim originally, and the green *verdigris* paint pigment did contain copper acetate and was deadly poisonous.

Members of De Soto's men were in the Ozarks in the mid 1500's. *Arguebuses* were predecessors to muskets, were muzzle loaders and used black powder. Casqui were a real tribe in that time.

In 1764 Liguest established a trading post at what would become St. Louis. The French name *La Riviere Courante* was Anglicized to Current River. Had it been translated, we would be floating Running River.

Charleville muskets were one of the better long barreled firearms in use leading up to the Revolutionary War. *Boucherons* were French made trade knives. In 1731, the knife maker from Solinger, Germany registered his brand and Henckels still today is known for its quality cutlery. The *D'Anville* map carried by the fictitious Beaumont was drawn in 1732 and published in 1752. Previously the *Carte de la Lousiana et du Cour du Mississippi* by Guillaume Delisle published in 1718 best emphasized French interests as the London cartographer Herman Moll accentuated the British claims when published in 1720. Early maps were not only frequently works of art but often simplistic attempts at propaganda. These maps with such divergent representations were national attempts to claim more territory for their respective countries as Great Britain and France were in disagreement over sovereignty of the Ohio Valley.

Osage and Caddo tribes did frequently fight throughout numerous parts of the Ozarks.

The Panic of 1819 was in fact America's first economic crisis. Much like the South Sea Bubble financial disaster of a century before, it too was the result of rampant speculation and close ties to the economy of Europe. Cotton prices fell 25% in one single day.

There really was a group called the Secret Order of the Sons of Liberty. They were among several groups that organized for the purpose of promoting civil unrest. Some did so for the continuation of illegal activities by which they were profiting; others refused to accept the outcome of the War. Many were dedicated to protecting the lands of friends and family that were being purchased by "Northerners." They disrupted tax sales and even burned out and killed to prevent new ownership. The State Immigration Act of 1865 did solicit immigration at the end of the Civil War, as there had been a significant reduction of the population—some from death, many from the exodus from the state due in great part to the state of lawlessness. From 1860 to 1870, corn production in Missouri was down 6% and cattle production 25%.

Alley Springs and the mill, as well as the community, were named after the Alley Family who at the time were one of the larger landowners.

The Table

Wife Judy still has some two-inch lumber from such a tree that I did cut up for a neighbor. I strive to handle adversity as well as the fictitious Paul, for Judy is the equal of the fictitious Jenny in grace, beauty and ingenuity.

The Picture

Based on a true encounter in the Missouri Botanical Garden the fall of 2013.

Grandpa's New Book

Inspired merely by a chance reading of the scripture in King James and comparing it to the New International Version from which I generally study.

The Bucket List

An extension of one of my columns—*Reflections from the Road.*

The Blizzard Brunch

Sadly, ninety-percent true. Even the names. The Moss family are great friends.

The Gift

Based on my real experiences of driving a fuel truck. I do have a friend who does own a small oil business. The request is fictitious, for in real life the vast majority of exchanges of favors are he and his family to me and mine.

Check #1817

This a very real story, and a truly wonderful young lady. We still have the check, and the card.

What's In A Name?

This is the version told by a family that grew up just upriver from the Bunch Place. Both hog related stabbings were real occurrences.

The Pay Check

See above. If not for pulmonary challenges, this would have been the best job I ever held. Customers were farmers and small businesses, with a lot of them in the timber industry.

Grandma's New Pet

Inspired by a mother who loves cats and sadly is losing her vision. Yes, I know…………..

A Half Century of Hunting Tails

Very real, including the names. Inspired by some very bittersweet memories. The cabin is still on Blairs Creek and the wall is still accumulating shirt tails. Art has passed.

American Heroes---"Ozark Fisherman Saves the Day"

All true, including there being a Blazer Boat Manufacturer in Ellington, Missouri. An interesting addendum, when this was published as both jest and tribute; a local business called and offered to sponsor the next episode. Blazer Boats is the major sponsor of the very real Ozarks Heritage Project. Jack Roberts and his family remain cherished friends.

A Riverman's Legacy

Please be sure and read the dedication at the front of the book. This story is completely true, told to me by a firsthand witness to the events. I barely knew Buck Maggard, but have the honor of calling two of his children good friends. Eugene of Aker's Ferry Canoe Rental and Judy Stewart of Riverside Motel and Cabins in Eminence.

The Stand

Based on a similar experience with the Art from A Half Century of Hunting Tails. Over the years, Art went to great lengths to put me on some fine deer crossings. Once, I arrived at a crossing to which he'd given me directions, and found he'd stowed a metal folding chair in nearby brush for my comfort. Art Cook was a very dear friend.

He honored me several years after this event by asking me to preach his funeral, explaining that he had little use for preachers. When I offered that in truth I preached, though not for money, he explained as follows. "You preach some, that's true. But you don't take money. Growing up out here in the country, we had young girls that saved themselves for marriages, but a lot chose not to. 'Gave it away' if you will. That might have been slutty behavior; but as long as they never took money, we had no cause to call them whores. You ain't no preacher!"

The Check

Based on a very true incident a few years back. When the story was written, I'd already forgotten for sure which choice I had in fact made. I fear I cashed it.

Healing Waters

Historically accurate, including the naval battles. Dr. Diehl was real, the other characters imagined. Now is a wonderful stretch of river to fish, particularly in the winter.

Fifty Dollars

Fiction. I did do a fair amount of boxing in my much younger days. Mostly for fun, occasionally for side bets. The Hill is real, and where in my youth I frequently ran.

The Deadline

As a weekly newspaper columnist, I have too often felt this fear. The story was based on one of hundreds of daydreams about some such event coming to my rescue.

The Pavilion

Based quite closely on a true story. The Pavilion may be seen at Pilgrim's Rest Cemetery off Highway 19 in northern Shannon County, or on facebook Pilgrim's Rest Cemetery Association.

The Legend of Ol '95

Fiction, obviously; but inspired by experiences lived during more than two decades of hauling canoes on Current River.

The Ghost Mule

Based loosely on a story I heard as a child. Many of the older members of the community of Timber in which I grew up were of some degree of Native American linage. Others had Irish blood; several both. Legends of both cultures worked their way into stories told over fires in the dark of night. A pale, or white, animal was frequently associated with death in these cultures.

Secrets of Horse Hollow

There really is a Horse Hollow on Jacks Fork and there are numerous hard to find caves in the surrounding area. This story was inspired by tales of a worker at a summer camp that did enjoy scaring children. Unfortunately, the one about the little girl being found frozen was based on a real event; names obviously changed.

In gathering tales, I have encountered older people who routinely refer to "secrets that don't need told." Often they are tied to a specific geographical entity and hint at the supernatural.

A Casket's True Calling

My father, Tudor Nichols Mansfield, worked at the Salem radio station recording advertisements. This would have been in the early 1960's; he even crossed paths with Mitch Jayne during some of that time. Somehow the station owner found himself with two coffins, most likely settlement in lieu of cash. My father became the owner of one, most likely from a similar arrangement. The visit from the law was quite real. As was Earl the edgerman. His name was Earl Goforth and he was truly a master of his craft. He did have an older relative, not sibling, named Cecil. Therein lies an anthology of tales.

The Pie Supper

A fictional event and imaginary characters. The custom itself quite real. I have had the honor of auctioneering and emceeing such events for forty-plus years. This is one of my favorite stories. Many names borrowed from some wonderful people.

A Petition Remembered

Again, imagination inspired by experience. As of this writing I have performed more than two dozen marriages and spoken at sixty funerals. I started helping to hand dig graves before a teenager. Tony Weber, the same older mentor who instigated my career as an auctioneer, also started me grave digging. He did take a framing square, the "L" shaped thing, as well as a sharp double-bit axe to all such projects. Though there is a graveyard named Lone Pine, the majority of our work was done in the Weese Cemetery a few miles further north. He was quite adamant about the quality of such efforts. I helped hand dig my last grave just a few years ago. Ironically, it was for Tony's son-in-law.

I believe it a real shame that this practice is coming to an end, as I have found it extremely cathartic and a wonderful way to remember and honor someone's life.

Moonlight Memories

Echo Bluff is quite real, and quite beautiful. It is part of the Camp Zoe land seized by our government and is about to become part our state park system. I have fished it alone and with family and friends, and originally with my father. The vast majority of what we caught were released unharmed.

I preached my father's funeral February of 2009. There are times I very much feel his presence.

The Call of the ……….Couch?

Mostly true. The three miniature bluetick beagles were named Little Miss Daisy, named after the neighbor's bluetick pup; her sister Dharma and brother Huck. When she was about 10 months old we acquired Daisy, who became Big Daisy. D for short. D still runs rabbits during the day and trees the occasional raccoon at night. Last winter she was so excited the night she had a sow and three kittens up the same large water oak; she stayed treed for more than three hours when I finally went and led her home.

The one thing the fictional Shelly and Calvin had wrong was they did not have the rest of their lives to train the "tuppies." Miss Daisy had to be put down in October of 2010 because of kidney failure; Huck met the same fate January of 2014.

The Intervention

More about the same Big D. The intervention didn't work. Pretty well have had the same experience with people.

Oh, What A Name!

The names have been somewhat changed to protect the innocent. This is based on a real family story passed down from generation to generation to explain the uniqueness of their family surname. I added a bit of a twist at the end.

Great Expectations---Ozark Style

My salute to the genius that was Charles Dickens (this title is ALL you will find in this book reminiscent of that great author). True story with a few name changes. I can still see the look on her face when confronted that night with my paltry offering. As always, the couple was still extremely appreciative.

The Handshake

True story and a valuable lesson for all, especially that part about eye contact.

Rainbow Springs

Real places, both here and across the waters. The battles mentioned all too real, the casualty numbers staggering. Many from the rural Ozarks fought in these wars, quite a few did not make it home and those that did often were never quite the same. Historically many cultures have legends of healing waters, including that of the Celts. Stumbling across an old Irish tale gave birth to this one. The original tale used constellations to guide one to healing waters. Our twist was a spring that addressed a specific need as well as utilizing the rainbow to find it.

A River's Cries

Taken almost directly from an editorial written by Judy (Maggard) Stewart, daughter of Buck Maggard to whom this work is dedicated. Believed it fitting to close with her quite inspirational observations. In fairness, some of the land acquired in the late 1960's by the National Park Service for the creation of the Ozark National Scenic Riverways was voluntarily sold by a few families. Much was taken through the process of eminent domain. Many beautiful farm houses and community schools were destroyed, as was a wonderful lodge building at Round Springs.

As this book goes to print, the NPS/ONSR is in the process of drafting their new General Management Plan that could guide this area for the next twenty years. Ironically, much of the 1984 GMP currently in effect has yet to be implemented.

I hope you enjoyed the stories, appreciated the clarification. It has been my pleasure supplying both. Our organization, the Ozark Heritage Project, was founded to preserve the Ozark culture as well as the physical environment. We host several river cleanings annually as well as present aspects of this culture in person and in writings. Our efforts can be followed at www.ozarkheritageproject.org   Thanks!

Dr. Eric "Rick" Mansfield is a retired educator who writes the weekly column *Reflections from the Road* for several local newspapers. Rick is co-founder and president of the Ozark Heritage Project, a non-profit organization dedicated to the preservation and restoration of Ozark culture and the inspiration of future generations to do likewise. OHP sponsors river and stream clean-ups as well as hosts and co-hosts numerous outdoor events.

Rick does storytelling, often in character, and is always looking for new audiences. Rick and his wife Judy, who does woodworking and quilting, live on a small organic farm with their two remaining dogs—Dharma, a miniature bluetick beagle, and Daisy, an eighty-five pound bluetick coonhound. They all enjoy the outdoors. Rick may be reached at 701 CR 602, Ellington, MO 63638 or emansfield2004@yahoo.com .

Made in the USA
Monee, IL
12 June 2023